DEADLY KNIGHT

MIDNIGHT EMPIRE: THE TOWER, BOOK 3

ANNABEL CHASE

RED PALM PRESS LLC

1

Kamikaze Marwin trudged up a set of concrete steps in central Britannia City. "You would think people would be happy about a tree sprouting in the middle of the city. Maybe we can hang those cute little lights on the branches and make it festive."

"Let's see what we're dealing with first," I warned. "Normal trees don't grow in the middle of the city." And they certainly didn't bust straight through a fountain and send statues flying like oversized shrapnel.

Kami kicked aside a pebble. "Normal trees don't grow anywhere anymore."

She wasn't wrong. Nature suffered after the Great Eruption, a cataclysmic event that involved ten of the world's supervolcanoes blowing their stacks simultaneously. The expulsion of ash left the world shrouded in darkness which took a catastrophic toll on Mother Nature. Without sunlight, most plant life became reliant on magic to grow and thrive.

We crested the steps and Kami released a whistling breath. "Blimey Charlie. That's quite a tree."

No kidding. It stood over sixty feet high and had a

circumference of at least thirty feet. Thick branches twisted from the trunk like broken arms reaching for restoration. Wisps of powerful magic brushed against my skin. Even without the magical hint, it was obvious this was no ordinary tree.

"It's a Parijata tree."

Kami cast a sideways glance at me. "Am I supposed to know what that is?"

"A wishing tree. My mother told me it yields objects of desire." If anyone would know the background of the Parijata tree, it was dearly departed Rhea Hayes, beloved mother and history teacher extraordinaire.

Kami's eyebrows lifted. "Any limits?"

"None that I know of."

She regarded the tree. "Huh. So I can ask the tree to restore the sun and bam!" She slapped her palms together. "Instant rays of light."

"Okay, maybe there are some limits. I'm pretty sure the wish has to be for you personally."

"Still seems too good to be true. What does the tree get out of it?"

Kami and I had fought enough monsters to know that magic gifts often came with a price tag. The greater the gift, the heftier the cost.

"The wishes feed the tree. The more wishes there are, the bigger the tree grows. The next thing you know, you've got a tree the size of a city block and a root system that destroys everything in its path. Farewell Britannia City." What was left of it. The city wasn't fully rebuilt after the Great Eruption. The Eternal Night took hold and bye-bye infrastructure.

Kami's shoulders sagged. "A huge tree and here's me without my power saw. We should've stopped by a hardware store. All I have on me is a crossbow."

"No worries. First order of business is to clear the area. The tree only grows stronger if we let people continue to make wishes."

"Please don't feed the tree." Kami started to usher people out of the way. "The wish factory is closed. The genie has left the building."

An elderly man turned toward us, eyes flashing. "I'm not going anywhere, young lady. This is my chance."

"Your chance to what?" Kami asked.

"Reclaim my youth," he shot back. "What else?"

Kami and I exchanged glances.

"This isn't the Fountain of Youth, sir," I said. It wasn't even a decorative water fountain anymore. The opportunistic tree took care of that.

"I'm wishing to be young again, you fool," he snapped.

Kami gave him a heavy dose of side-eye. "So you can learn to be a grumpy old man all over again? Don't do the world any favors."

A woman pushed through the throng of people wearing a bright smile. "My teeth!" She ran her tongue over the straight, white squares. "Are they as perfect as they feel?"

I nodded. "They look like they belong on a billboard."

She beamed. "I can't wait to show my husband. Maybe now he'll stop calling me Bucky." She dashed off to display her good fortune.

"Sounds like she should've wished for a divorce," Kami muttered.

Another branch sprouted from the trunk of the tree, this one even higher than the last.

"We need to stop this now," I said.

Kami tipped her head back to examine the tree's new height. "It's already pretty big. How do we get rid of it?"

I sensed the growing agitation around us at the sight of two knights. No surprise. They knew why we were here. Funny thing about people—they tended to dislike the idea of someone destroying their hopes and dreams. If Kami and I weren't careful, the tree would turn the crowd against us as a protective measure.

"You take care of the bystanders and I'll deal with the tree," I told her.

Kami's specialty was mind control. Although she couldn't commandeer dozens of people at once, she could quietly manipulate one head at a time and steer them away from the scene.

"Hey," Kami called to the tree. "Make like a...you and leave."

The tree remained rooted in place.

Kami sighed. "If we're going to kill it anyway, would it be so bad to make one teensy wish?"

I jerked toward my best friend. "Don't you even consider it, Kamikaze Marwin. You and I have magic. It would be like using extra-strength fertilizer." Feeding the tree my powerful and unpredictable magic would be a huge mistake. There was no telling what my wish would do to the tree—or to the city. The gods knew I had plenty of wishes to make, but I couldn't afford to be selfish. Not ever.

Begrudgingly Kami turned to the woman next to her and set to work. I focused on the tree and came up with a basic plan. Minimal damage to the property. Minimal damage to the people. Permanent damage to the tree.

Easy peasy, right?

I removed my trusty axe from the sheath on my back and debated where to strike first. Babe was my weapon of choice and not a bad option under the circumstances.

A young woman spotted the axe and grabbed her child's

hand to tug her away from me. "What are you doing with that?" the woman demanded. Her complexion was milky white except for the dark circles under her eyes.

"The tree is dangerous," I said. "I suggest you take your child and evacuate the area." There was every chance the tree would fight back and I didn't want some poor kid getting a concussion due to a flying branch.

The young woman tightened her grip on the child's hand. "We're not going anywhere until I get my wish."

"Mum, we should go," the child urged. "The knight says it's dangerous."

The mother ignored her child's plea and kept her focus on me. "I've been sick. If this tree can cure me, then we're staying put. I won't leave Sasha an orphan if I can help it."

I glanced at the child and resisted the memories that their predicament stirred. I understood the woman's desire. I'd been older than Sasha when my mother died, but that didn't make the road to adulthood any easier. A child as young as Sasha would likely die in this city without a caretaker.

"Make your wish quickly and go," I said. The sick woman was human. Her wish wouldn't give the tree too much juice.

I pivoted back to the tree and chose an easy branch to test first. One good whack and a branch broke off and fell to the pavement, splintering into pieces.

I glanced up at the rest of the tree and sighed. "One down. Too many to count to go."

"What are you doing?" a heavyset man demanded. "I'm about to make a wish."

"I'm aware of that, sir. I'm trying to save you from yourself."

He sneered at me. "I don't need some woman telling me

what to do. I've been wanting revenge on my ex-wife for years and this tree is going to get it for me."

Before he had a chance to make his wish, I knocked him on the back of the head with the blunt end of my axe. He slumped to the ground.

"Kami, I helped you with this one!"

I turned to the tree. I had to hurry or I'd be fighting off an angry mob. If somebody in the crowd was really smart, they'd wish me harm so I couldn't take away their precious tree.

As I raised the axe for another round of whack-a-branch, the tree sprouted two new limbs at once. What on earth?

I whirled around to see Sasha and her mother still in the vicinity of the tree. A pinkish hue had returned to the young woman's cheeks and her dark circles had vanished.

"But you're human," I said, confused.

"I am, but she isn't." The young woman squeezed her daughter's hand.

Of course. How could I have expected a child that age to resist making a wish? Lesson learned.

"You both need to go. Now."

A brown pony burst through the crowd of onlookers, mane flying like a mud-covered flag, and halted in front of the mother and daughter.

Sasha brightened. "It worked!"

The kid wished for a freakin' pony.

Because of course she did.

Mother and daughter climbed onto the pony's back and off they went.

"Unbelievable," Kami said, watching the pony trot down the steps.

"I know, right?"

She continued to stare at the vacant steps. "Why didn't I think of a pony?"

I groaned. "You can have Trio. She's as big as a pony." The three-headed canine monstrosity I'd rescued from the tunnels had taken up residence at the Pavilion, the Knights of Boudica headquarters, and now worked as a security guard dog.

"Too much slobber." Kami contemplated the tree. "I don't think my crossbow is going to be much help to you unless you want me to launch tranquilizer darts at people."

"If it comes to it," I said.

"Looking for one of these?" another voice said.

Fellow knight Briar Niall appeared behind us holding a chainsaw.

"My hero," Kami declared. "How did you know?"

"Minka told me to bring one to this address." Briar switched it on, pulled the rope a couple times, and a motor sprang to life.

Kami moved swiftly. She snatched the chainsaw from an unsuspecting Briar and raced to the lowest branch of the tree.

"Hey, no fair!" Briar called after her. "Now I don't have a weapon."

"You *are* a weapon," I told her.

Briar glanced down at her dark blue suit of magical armor. "Fair enough. At least I came dressed for the occasion." She observed Kami now sawing off a sturdy branch. "I should probably ask why we're destroying a perfectly nice tree."

"Because it isn't perfectly nice," I said. "It will destroy this entire block by the end of the day."

"So it's basically my nephew after ingesting a bag of candy."

"Get in there, Briar. We're wasting time."

I backed away and a fur-covered monster exploded from the suit. No one would guess the creature Briar was capable of unleashing. As the only shapeshifter in our banner, she was a valuable member of the team, especially during times like this when we needed brute strength. Nobody could identify her species—not even Briar herself. We only knew that, when she turned, she was a walking, talking terror.

Briar rushed to the trunk of the tree, acting as a battering ram. In her case, size mattered. Bark crunched as she threw her impressive body weight against the tree for a second time.

Kami switched to attacking the roots now threaded through the concrete and I used my earth magic to loosen the roots from the ground. It felt good to release a bit of magic. No one knew the pressure I was under to contain the full extent of my magic. I had to shift the lid and let the steam out of my magic pot every now and again or I'd boil over. If that ever happened, I'd scald anyone within range.

A familiar bird swooped down from the sky to land on a tree branch.

"Barnaby, that isn't a good spot to rest," I yelled.

The raven cawed in response but remained perched on the branch. Stubborn bird. A pair of gray pigeons followed Barnaby's lead and landed on another branch.

I made a sweeping gesture. "No birds!"

The tree shook as Briar struck the trunk for a third time.

The raven held fast.

I used our telepathic connection to warn him away. He spread his wings and flew overhead just as Briar prepared for a fourth strike. She stood upright on powerful haunches and yowled. The primal sound sent shivers down my spine. Briar was the most docile woman alive in her human form.

You half expected a parade of children to follow her around in the city, their sweet voices raised in song. In her beast form, though, she was a verifiable nightmare.

Briar struck again and the trunk of the tree split apart and collapsed on either side of the base.

Kami switched off the saw as the roots shriveled and dissipated. "Is it wrong that I'm disappointed?"

Briar reverted to her human form and smoothed the front of her creased uniform. "I am so grateful Minka invested in these. They make shifting so easy."

"Don't tell Minka," Kami advised. "It'll go to her head."

Briar observed the remains of the tree. "We should gather the wood and donate it."

I heaved a weary sigh. "I wish we could, but it's unusable. You toss a piece of this on a fire and inadvertently make a wish, and you'll have a problem on your hands."

"That's too bad." Briar nudged a piece of the broken tree with her boot. "What do we do with it then?"

"We should burn it now while nobody's within range." I didn't need magic for this task. I simply used two pieces of wood as kindling and rubbed them together until they sparked.

"I don't suppose anyone's packing marshmallows," Kami said. "Seems like a waste of a good fire."

"Whatever you do, don't wish for them," I said.

As I watched the tree burn, I felt a pang of loss. It seemed sacrilege to deliberately destroy the tree even though I knew it was for the best.

"Mission accomplished," Kami declared.

"If only I felt better about it." The wood crackled and popped as it turned to ash.

Kami hooked her arm through mine. "At least our job is fun. How many people can say that?"

I glanced at her, incredulous. "Your mind works in mysterious ways."

She gave me an innocent look. "What?"

I waved a hand at the remains of the tree. "It isn't fun to crush people's hopes and dreams."

Briar scooped the chainsaw off the ground. "I'll take this back to the office. Are you two coming?"

"That depends," Kami said. "Is Minka there?"

"She was when I left. She made me stop to sign out the chainsaw."

I laughed. "Of course she did."

"We have another stop to make, but we'll be there shortly," Kami said.

I waited until Briar was out of earshot to turn to her. "We will?"

"No, but she can tell Minka and buy us time before we get the dreaded phone call requesting our location."

"Where are we going until then?"

Kami smiled. "How about a drink? We just saved the city like proper superheroes. That calls for a celebration."

I narrowed my eyes. "What's the real reason?"

She hesitated. "Can't fool you, can I?"

"Nope."

"You've seemed a bit mopey."

"I haven't been mopey."

"You didn't pet Trio when you came to work yesterday. Major red flag." She studied me. "Thought you might want to talk, just the two of us."

"What do you mean? I talk to you all the time."

Kami groaned. "Not about important things like feelings and whatnot."

"That's not true. I'm an open book."

She snorted. "Only if that open book is closed, locked,

warded, and buried underground in the middle of the Sahara."

"That's not an open book."

"And neither are you. Is it something to do with Callan?"

I held my breath. I'd been trying very hard not to think about the vampire prince. "I don't know what you mean. We worked together. The job finished. End of story." I started walking. Maybe if I walked fast enough, she'd get distracted and change the subject. Kami was squirrel-like in her commitment to topics of conversation.

"Admit it. You two have a connection." She hurried to catch up to me. So much for my squirrel theory.

"We did not connect in any way, shape, or form." A bald-faced lie, but it was a hill I was willing to die on.

"You made out with him, didn't you?"

I refused to satisfy her curiosity.

"I knew it! Tongue or no tongue? Who am I kidding? He's a royal vampire. Of course there was tongue. Fangs, too. Did they tickle or hurt so good?"

I glared at her. "Are we fifteen again? Seriously, Kami. Drop it." I didn't want to talk about him. I hadn't heard from Callan since he fled my flat and told me to stay away from him because my life was at stake. I'd never had a guy go to such great lengths to break up with me—not that we'd technically been dating. One intense lip session does not a relationship make.

"Sorry." She offered a sheepish grin. "What if drinks are on me? Are we good?"

Of course we were good. Kami was my best friend. She'd throw herself in front of a zombie horde to save me. Not many people were fortunate enough to have a friend like Kami.

I managed a weak smile. "Always."

2

Kami and I left the pub in better spirits than when we entered, which was basically the point.

"Neera said things are going well with Roxanne," Kami said. "I feel bad for Ione." Neera and Ione Sheehan were sisters skilled in earth magic. Both knights, they tended to work together on assignments.

"Why would you feel bad for Ione? She didn't want to date Roxanne."

"No, but she's used to spending a lot of time with her older sister. She seems bummed."

"I think this is good for Ione. She leans on Neera too much. It'll force her out of her comfort zone."

"They probably say that about us, too." Kami squinted across the street. "What's happening over there?"

I followed her gaze to a gathering crowd. Bodies huddled together with their backs to us, intent on something I couldn't see.

"Not sure," I said.

"If it's another tree, I call dibs on the saw."

"I need a higher vantage point." I climbed onto a partial

stone wall and drew myself to a standing position. Four vampires in royal uniforms flanked someone in a black hood. He wore a sleeveless shirt and his brown trousers were ripped and soiled. My stomach clenched when I spotted the copper bowl at their feet.

"Can you see anything?" Kami asked.

Unfortunately I could. "It's a public execution."

"Shit." Kami joined me on the crumbling wall.

One of the royal representatives stepped forward. His red cape flapped in the breeze. Even from this distance, his fangs appeared exceptionally long and the cruel slant of his mouth suggested he would enjoy what he was about to do.

I strained to listen to his announcement. "...James Thornhill has been tried and convicted of section 32(a) of the penal code."

Thanks to my job, I knew that section well. No subject is permitted to perform magic unless the act falls under one of the exceptions, such as working as a knight in pursuit of an official objective.

"By order of King Casek, we condemn this wizard to death." The vampire used a ceremonial dagger to slice open a vein in each of the man's arms.

I shifted uncomfortably at the mention of the king. It was hard to reconcile the kindly vampire with a ruler who would demand a public execution for a minor crime. Then again, King Casek didn't earn his place on the throne by being soft. Even if his former wife, Queen Britannia, had been the more ruthless and violent half of the couple, she died twenty years ago. There was no reason to do things her way now. I knew what Callan would say, though. If House Lewis's control of magic started to slip, vampires worried that witches and wizards would garner enough strength to overthrow vampire rule. Outlawing magic made it easier to maintain a balance. Even the use of Latin was illegal unless such use fell under one of the limited exceptions. The former queen's paranoia had seeped into the law of the land.

We watched as blood slid down the wizard's wounds and collected in the bowl. I knew where that blood would end up and it sickened me.

Kami turned away. "This is barbaric. They're making a spectacle of his death."

I didn't disagree, but it seemed wrong to avert my gaze. I felt a strange sense of obligation to observe the devastating conclusion to this wizard's life.

"They want to use him as a cautionary tale." They'd probably stick his head on a spike at Tower Bridge. An additional deterrent to criminal behavior for all those who missed the execution itself.

Kami's expression was grim. "Consider me cautioned."

"The sun shall once again rise," the wizard bellowed. His voice cracked on the last syllable.

Kami jumped to the pavement. "I can't watch anymore."

The tightening of the rope jerked his head backward. His hood slipped down to reveal a bright yellow star tattooed on his bald head. For a stunned moment, I thought of Joseph Yardley, otherwise known as the Green Wizard and the ringleader of the People in Support of Ra. Yardley and his band of followers were dedicated to bringing back the sun and banishing vampires to the shadows again.

I shook off the shock. I already knew it wasn't Yardley. This wizard was named James Thornhill.

The vampire to the left kicked the crate from beneath the wizard's feet. Thornhill twisted like a sheet in the wind. Despite the tightness of the noose, his neck failed to snap. His fingers clawed at the rope around his neck. It was nauseating to watch. I couldn't save him, but I couldn't let him suffer. No crime deserved such inhumane treatment.

Turning invisible, I jumped to the pavement. I maneuvered quickly through the crowd and hopped on the discarded crate.

"Sleep well, friend," I whispered in his ear.

It took only seconds to snap the wizard's neck and relieve his pain. To the onlookers it simply appeared that the rope had done its job.

I darted back to the wall where a red-faced Kami awaited me.

"Are you out of your mind?" she seethed. "Do you not see the complete lunacy of doing the exact thing that got that man killed?"

"Technically I didn't use magic." My invisibility came from my vampire side. "Besides, no one saw me."

Kami gaped at me. "Sometimes I want to throat-punch you for sheer stupidity." She exhaled. "And then I want to hug you for your compassion."

We made ourselves scarce before the crowd started to disperse. No need to get caught in the tangled web of arms and legs.

"Emotions are complex," I remarked once we were out of harm's way.

"I bet you've been saying that a lot lately," Kami said with a knowing look.

I glared back at her. "You did *not* just circle back to the topic I told you to drop."

"I thought the ale might loosen your lips. I can see I was mistaken."

I gestured to the left. "I'm not going to the office. You can complete the paperwork for the tree."

"Gee, thanks. You know how much I love ticking Minka's boxes."

"That sounds dirty."

She shrugged. "I can make anything sound dirty. That's my real superpower. Where are you headed?"

"Library. I have research to catch up on."

She shook her head. "You and books. I think you would've been happier as a librarian."

She wasn't wrong, except the library technically belonged to the royal family and I swore I'd never work for vampires. Of course I broke my own rule when I accepted a job for House Lewis that involved rescuing Princess Davina from a kidnapper and retrieving a powerful stone chock full of elemental magic. That was how I'd met Callan. The prince wasn't a member of House Lewis by birth. That honor went to House Duncan, the ruling family in Scotland. King Glendon lost his bid for power twenty years ago during the Battle of Britannia and lost his only son and heir as well. The peace treaty required Callan to be raised in Britannia City as a ward of House Lewis. Although Callan was no longer a boy, there was still a decade to go on his House's promise.

I took a bus across town and entered the lobby of the Britannia Library. The sprawling institution was one of the better preserved buildings in the city. Not all royal vampire families were as supportive of books and museums as House Lewis. Now that I'd met them personally, I found myself wavering in my blanket objection to vampires.

Of course there was still the small problem of their desire to kill my species. As a dhampir, I was more of a threat to vampires than anyone. My mother, a skilled witch, taught me everything she knew before her untimely death. She also taught me to keep my species secret. A dhampir would be executed on sight—no questions asked. That was how hated we were.

How hated I was.

I was disappointed to see Adelaide behind the counter. Pedro Gutierrez was my preferred Head Librarian. The witch usually ducked when she saw me coming, whereas Pedro had more patience when it came to my unique requests.

To her credit, Adelaide remained in an upright position today and even managed a friendly smile. "Welcome back to the library, Miss Hayes. Always a pleasure."

I drummed my fingers on the counter. "No Pedro today?"

"No. He and Garrison are off. How may I be of service?" She was a short, stout woman with exceptionally broad shoulders that she kept covered with a shawl that looked like it had been knitted together by blind mice. Her dirt-brown hair was cropped close to her head. In the right light, it resembled a large, wet oak leaf.

I glanced around to make sure no one was eavesdropping. "I'd like any information you have on Friseal's Temple."

She pursed her lips. "A temple, you say? Can you spell the name, please? I'm not familiar with it."

I spelled Friseal and waited as she used her magic to scan the inventory for matches. She wrote a list of titles and catalogue numbers and slid it across the counter to me.

"I'm afraid there isn't much, but these might help."

Thanking her, I glanced at the list. Three books. There was a good chance the temple wasn't even the main subject. It was more likely that the books only included passing references.

I was fairly certain I heard a sigh of relief as I turned to walk away. No surprise. More than once Adelaide had been subjected to inquiries that involved real-life examples by me —some of which may have involved blood and guts. It wasn't my fault she was squeamish. In my defense, I always cleaned up whatever mess I made. What I couldn't do was wipe Adelaide's memory clean.

I located the first section on the list and disappeared between the stacks. I had a religious-like reverence for knowledge. Queen Britannia had destroyed all the churches during her reign but thankfully left libraries intact. One of my favorite smells in the world was the earthy combination of leather and paper. I took a moment to inhale the scent before I started the search.

Friseal's Temple was quite possibly the key to unlocking the mystery of a set of powerful stones that had recently been discovered. Each stone contained immense power related to a specific supernatural ability. The Immortality Stone was already in the possession of House Lewis and had been for centuries. The family didn't realize there were similar stones until the discovery of the Elemental Stone, which led to Davina's kidnapping. Then the Transcendence Stone inadvertently arrived in the city from Devon. I wasn't sure whether these stones had official names, but I'd given them my own. A museum curator named Antonia Birch had used the term 'transcendence' in connection with the stone that influenced shapeshifting, so I'd adopted the name. Antonia had paid dearly for sharing her knowledge with me.

I located the first book on the list and tugged it from its place on the shelf. I flipped straight to the index and there it was. Friseal's Temple. Perfect. I leafed through the book until I reached the right page.

Except the right page was missing.

I double-checked the page numbers. Sure enough, pages

135 and 136 were missing. Terrific. Of all the pages for vandals to mess with, it had to be those two.

I tucked the book under my arm and continued to the next section. I'd show the damaged book to Adelaide on my way out of the library and swear I had nothing to do with it. I'd sooner break my own arm than damage a library book.

Unfortunately the search for the second book yielded similar results. There was only one reference to Friseal's Temple and it had been removed from the book as well. I'd assumed the first book was a case of bad luck. The second book was making me rethink that assumption.

The third book confirmed my suspicions.

I delivered all three damaged books to the counter. Adelaide sucked in a horrified breath when I showed her the missing pages.

"Is there a way to find out when this happened or who might have tampered with them?"

Adelaide mulled over the questions. "I can check with Garrison and Pedro and see whether anyone else requested them recently. We don't keep records of walk-in requests like yours, so I'd have to rely on their memories."

I figured as much. "Why take the pages and not the books?" The pages made it obvious that someone was trying to hide information.

"The books would've set off an alarm, but the pages aren't individually protected."

That made sense. "Will you let me know what you find out?"

"Absolutely." Adelaide frowned at the torn pages. "What do you know about this temple?"

"Aside from the fact that someone wants to keep the information hidden, not very much." I wasn't about to tell her about the stones or the death of poor Antonia Birch, the museum curator. Adelaide would never want to help me again.

The witch closed the books and stacked them in a pile. "I'll be sure to contact you if I learn anything."

"Thank you. I appreciate it."

Just once it would be nice to have a straightforward request for poor Adelaide. Then again, every job came with a downside and it seemed I was Adelaide's.

I RETURNED to my flat and maneuvered around the tiny kitchen. I scooped food into bowls for five eager faces that I affectionately referred to as 'the menagerie.' There was a red panda called Big Red, a pygmy goat called Herman, a fennec fox named Sandy, Jemima the Bantam hen, and Hera, queen of 'cat-titude.' We had a mutually beneficial arrangement. The menagerie depended on me for survival and I depended on them for emotional support. When I was a terrified teenaged orphan living by my wits in the underground tunnels of Britannia City, animal companions saved my sanity. Kami's presence helped, of course—unlikely I would've survived without her—but there was no substitute for the affection of a furry friend.

Big Red scampered across the floor, matching my footsteps. The red panda suffered from separation anxiety even when I was inches away. I fed him last because I knew he'd be reluctant to leave my side.

Jemima clucked and pecked the seeds from the bowl. I'd removed the small hen's diaper before I fed her to give her feathered bottom a break. I only made her wear the diaper when I wasn't home to avoid a complete mess later.

A tapping sound drew me to the window that opened to a makeshift balcony. A flat on the top floor made it easier for me to let the animals in and out and avoid detection. Their presence violated my lease and I wasn't eager to become homeless again.

A pigeon lurked outside and I noticed the note tied to its leg. The last time a pigeon was out here, it was a royal carrier pigeon being held by Prince Callan, right before he told me he had to stay away from me.

This pigeon, however, was flying solo.

I unlocked the window and opened it. "Hello, friend. I take it you have a message for me."

I detached the note from its leg and the pigeon immediately flew away as though I'd removed the heavy weight that kept it grounded. I unfurled the note and recognized Pedro's small, neat handwriting.

No information here. Recommend Atheneum.

Wow. The Atheneum had an almost mythical status and was legendary among history buffs like my mother. Although she'd never been, she'd spoken of it with a reverence usually reserved for the gods.

The Atheneum meant a trip to Wales though. I'd only managed to cross into House Peyton territory with Callan's help. Wales was House Kane's territory and I'd need special dispensation to travel there. It was risky to go through official channels for approval if I was trying to hide my research trail. It would be best to seek an alternate method.

I knew firsthand that Callan owned a set of forged passports, one for him and one for a female companion. Maybe I could persuade him to lend me one again.

No.

I couldn't possibly ask a favor of him. Not when he'd made it clear he wanted to keep his distance from me. I'd have to find another way. Maybe Mack Quaid had a contact who could forge a passport. It wasn't something I'd needed before. As a knight I'd encountered my share of danger, but the powerful stones had elevated that danger to another level.

I picked up the phone and called Mack. The ringing sound was music to my ears. If the satellites weren't sending signals, I'd have to show up at his office in person and I wasn't in the mood for a long walk.

"Mack here."

"It's London."

"Hey, my favorite Knight of Boudica. Heard about the magic tree. Good job. Did you make a wish first? The knights in my office have a pool going."

"No wish."

"Yes!" I could practically hear his victorious fist pump. "Can I get that in writing from you? I'd like to collect my winnings before the weekend so I can take my wife somewhere nice for dinner."

"I'll take care of it. Listen, I need to take a trip to Wales. Know anybody who can make me a fake pass that passes muster?"

"Too tired of Minka's paperwork to do more?"

"Do I need to spell it out?"

"You don't want to be tracked, I get it. Why not?"

"You're nosy for a knight that specializes in confidential assignments."

"Passes are tough to come by, you know that. I only know one guy and I can't hook you up with a fake pass without knowing whether it might bite me in the ass later."

I sensed there was more to his hesitation than he was letting on. "What's the real issue?"

He sighed into the phone. "Now who's being nosy?"

"Come on. It's relevant."

"I suppose." He lowered his voice. "My contact helps relocate people out of the territory. Gives them a new start."

"Are we talking witness protection or something else?"

"Mainly refugees. People at risk for execution or at the top of the list for their local tribute center."

I sucked in a breath. Mack was involved in an Underground Railroad?

"Where do you send them?" Nowhere except South America was safe from vampire rule, but only because the continent had been taken over by monsters.

"Depends. If it's a tribute center issue, they only need to go to a nearby territory where they're not on a list."

"But House Lewis has reciprocal treaties with surrounding territories to return humans who dodge the list."

"You'd be surprised which Houses don't enforce that treaty."

Actually I wouldn't. "You send them to Devon, don't you?" The members of House Peyton hadn't seemed too excited to see Callan in their territory. Even though he was the heir to House Duncan, he was the ward of House Lewis and his presence seemed to rankle the royal household.

"I'd rather not say," Mack replied. "I have a system that works and I'm not too eager to put it at risk."

"Understandable. Not to worry, I'll find another way."

"Are you sure? You know I'd help you if I could."

"No, it's fine. I wouldn't want to jeopardize your operation. It's too important." My trip was important, too, but the risk was only to me rather than an entire group of vulnerable people.

"You're a good egg, London. A bit hard-boiled and covered in an impenetrable shell, but a good egg all the same."

"Sounds like you and Kami have been talking about me behind my back."

"And risk your wrath? Wouldn't dream of it."

"See you around, Mack."

I hung up the phone and sighed. It seemed I'd have to do this the old-fashioned way.

3

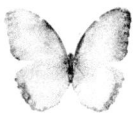

My efforts at sleep were thwarted by dreams I couldn't remember and I awoke feeling agitated and drenched in sweat. I must've experienced a surge of magic in response to my dreams and the flecks of silver that dotted my bare arms seemed to confirm my suspicion. I'd have to release a modicum of magic to ease the pressure.

I nudged Hera to join the other members of the menagerie at the foot of the bed. The cat didn't appreciate the gesture and hissed her displeasure before jumping to the floor.

I peeled back the sheet and said, "Levitas." My body rose a few inches and hovered over the bed. I called this the Goldilocks method—enough magic to relieve the buildup of energy but not so much that I collapsed in on myself like a dying star.

A dying star. That was the way I'd felt when I was on the rooftop of Romeo Rice's building facing off against a group of berserkers—werewolves that had lost control of their bodies as well as their minds. Romeo was a distinguished member of the tribunal for the West End Werewolf Pack—

at least he was until his untimely death in vampire custody. Romeo had taken possession of the Transcendence Stone after it made its way from Devon to our local pub, The Crown. Not realizing what the stone was but recognizing its power, Romeo had used it to experiment on members of his own pack with disastrous results. The trail had led me to Romeo's penthouse flat and the werewolf left me surrounded by his monstrous creations while he escaped with the stone. The fear and adrenaline I'd felt in that moment had triggered a surge of powerful magic like nothing I'd experienced before. Every day I fought to maintain control only to lose it in an explosion of silver light. Somehow the innocent werewolves had survived.

The outcome could've been much worse.

I watched with satisfaction as the silver faded. Good enough. I let myself drop to the bed and enjoyed the small bounce. I landed on my feet in front of the wardrobe. Herman stood in the doorway and bleated.

"I'm fine," I assured the pygmy goat.

Herman appeared unconvinced.

I opened the wardrobe and debated the options. If I wanted to secure permission to travel to Wales, it was best to present myself as an ordinary citizen and avoid drawing attention to myself. That meant swapping my Knight of Boudica magical armor for a black turtleneck sweater and dark jeans with black boots. A walking shadow.

The Passport Control Office was adjacent to the palace. I couldn't help but cast a furtive glance in the direction of the royal residence. There was no sign of Callan, not that I expected to see him.

Or cared.

Definitely didn't care.

I suppressed my vampire radar as I waited in the queue.

My dhampir status provided me with an internal alarm in connection with vampires. There was no need for alerts when I'd voluntarily placed myself in close proximity to them, though.

I checked my phone for messages. Nothing so far, which meant either a slow day at the office or a satellite malfunction. Hard to know which one until I spoke to Minka. Finally the vampire behind the counter signaled to me. My turn.

I stepped up to the counter and presented my identification as well as the completed travel form. As she scanned the paperwork, I noticed her left fang was slightly crooked. I winced, thinking how much more uncomfortable a crooked fang would be for the human if she opted to drink straight from the tap.

The vampire talked to herself under her breath and I couldn't decide whether this was her usual way of working or whether there was an issue. My impatience won out.

"Is there a problem?" I prompted.

Her gaze flicked from me to the papers in front of her. "My system says you're a Knight of Boudica."

"I am." So much for presenting myself as an ordinary citizen.

"Wonderful. I hired a knight once. Best money I ever spent."

"That's nice to hear. What was the problem?"

"There was a harpy terrorizing my street. Couldn't get the local council to do anything about it. They filed it under 'nuisance' and ignored it." She squared her shoulders. "Took it upon myself to raise the money and hire someone. Lovely gentleman by the name of Mack."

I jerked to attention. "Mack Quaid?"

The vampire's whole face brightened. "You know him?"

"We work together on occasion."

"You don't say." She took a renewed interest in me. "You must be good at your job if you work with Mack. He was top shelf." The vampire's expression soured. "Makes me sorry I can't approve your request."

I blanched. "Why not?"

"Your name is listed on the travel ban."

That was news to me. "*My* name? London Hayes?"

She nodded. "I've also been advised to report any attempt to travel to House Lewis."

My stomach clenched. "To anyone in particular?"

"I'm not at liberty to disclose that information."

I quickly debated my options. Making a scene didn't seem wise under the circumstances. I was trying to remain inconspicuous, not hold a blinking neon sign over my head.

Her gaze darted to the co-worker beside her and she dropped her voice. "Is this trip in connection with a job?"

"Yes," I said, matching her low tone. "Innocent lives are at stake."

She offered a solemn nod. "As far as I'm concerned, you were never here." The vampire slid the paperwork across the counter to me. "Tell Mack that Serena Howe says hello."

The knot in my stomach loosened. "Thank you, Serena." I shoved the papers in my pocket and left.

How on earth did I end up on the banned list? Prince Maeron had wanted eyes on me when I was working for the wolf pack, but that assignment was over now. He had no reason to stop me from traveling outside the territory. He didn't know I had the stones, nor did he know I was following a lead about Friseal's Temple.

Callan seemed unlikely as well. The Demon of House Duncan made it clear he wanted nothing to do with me. On that basis the farther away I was, the better.

I was so caught up in solving the mystery that I didn't register the tingling of my skin until I felt a hand grab my arm.

"London!"

I spun around to see Davina. The vampire princess smiled at me with a set of polished white fangs. Her blond curls were pinned to one side of her head like a young femme fatale and her porcelain skin was free of makeup aside from a swipe of black mascara that accentuated her eyes.

I bowed my head. "Your Highness, what a lovely surprise."

She swatted my arm. "You can stop with the formalities. Have you come to see us?"

"I was in the neighborhood on an errand."

Her laughter was infectious. "Don't be silly. We *are* the neighborhood. Come on." She tugged me toward the palace. "You can spare five minutes for the girl whose life you saved."

I knew there was no arguing with the stubborn princess. As sweet as the vampire was, she was also accustomed to getting her way.

My discomfort intensified as we bypassed the row of guards outside the palace. Any one of them could decide I was a threat that needed to be removed. They had carte blanche to act however they deemed fit. If I so much as looked at Davina the wrong way, they'd kill me on the spot.

"What have you been up to?" I asked, mostly to distract myself from the guards.

"No investigations if that's what you're asking. My parents have taken a hard stance on my extracurricular activities after the whole kidnapping debacle."

"I'm sorry," I said.

"Don't be sorry. There are still plenty of adventures in my future. Just not today."

We crossed the threshold into the palace, which only ratcheted up my natural defenses. My body screamed for me to turn and run. Although I knew Davina wasn't a threat, it was hard to ignore years of conditioning.

Of course, if Davina knew what I really was...That would be a different story.

"We'll chat in my study," Davina said.

"You have your own study?"

"Not really. It's where my lessons are held and I have another one in about five minutes." She turned a corner and I followed. "It's where all the children in the palace have been taught. I don't think it's been altered in decades."

The study was adorned with framed antique maps on the walls and rows of bookshelves. I couldn't help but think of my mother. She'd once stood in this very room. Not for very long—she'd only tutored the palace children for a brief time—but there was something thrilling about seeing the same room through her eyes. I'd take any excuse to feel close to her again.

Davina noticed my dazed expression. "You seem to find this study far more interesting than I do. Maybe you should sit for my lesson instead."

Reluctantly I broke my trance. "What can I say? I love books."

"I'd say you should've been a teacher, but a knight is much better."

"Much more dangerous, that's for sure," a voice said.

I kept a neutral expression plastered across my face as Callan joined us in the study. Dark blond hair. Sculpted jaw. Six feet and four inches of taut muscle. The vampire prince looked as perfect as ever, damn him. Couldn't he at least have the decency to grow a third arm or something?

"Look who it is, Callan," Davina said, full of the kind of cheer you'd expect of a teenaged princess without a care in the world. I envied her blithe nature.

Callan's gaze lingered on me. "What are you doing here? Did someone send for you?"

Davina smiled. "I ran into her outside the gates and insisted she pay us a visit."

If his green eyes were any more intense, they'd combust. "What were you doing outside the gates, may I ask?"

"Nothing exciting," Davina interjected. "Only an errand."

His brow furrowed. "What kind of errand involves the palace?"

"The kind that's none of your business and stop invading my privacy," I replied.

"I have no interest in your private matters, Miss Hayes. I was only being polite."

"You mean nosy."

Laughing, Davina sat at a desk and rested her chin on her knuckles. "I adore the way you two bicker."

We both looked at her. "We don't bicker," Callan said.

I held my index finger a millimeter away from my thumb. "We do a little bit."

Davina waved a hand. "Please carry on. I'm thoroughly entertained."

Callan's eyes twinkled. "Yes, sweet sister. Your entertainment was our intention. Don't you have a lesson soon?"

Davina groaned. "Don't remind me. Like I need to learn history."

"History is important," Callan told her. "What we fail to learn, we're doomed to repeat."

"I don't see the point of learning about those who ought to be relegated to footnotes. Kendall Masters is long dead and can't hurt us now. Why frighten us with her story?"

I flinched. Kendall Masters was the name my mother would trot out when she wanted to remind me of my fate should I slip and reveal myself.

"As far as I'm concerned this Kendall Masters is already a footnote," Callan said. "I don't even know who she is."

"And I don't know how you could forget her name," Davina countered. "She's the dhampir who managed to annihilate an entire village."

The seventeen-year-old had been groomed by her human uncle to become a trained killer of vampires. The girl's vampire father had abandoned his lover when he discovered she was pregnant. The mother had died in childbirth and the uncle chose to raise Kendall as his own, swearing vengeance. He honed the girl's unique skills and turned her into a weapon. He took her to the village where Kendall's paternal family lived and detonated her like a bomb.

Prior to the village massacre, Kendall had killed over forty vampires since the age of twelve, including her own father. When the vampires finally caught her, they didn't simply kill her. They tortured her slowly, in public, and forced her uncle to watch. Then they killed him too. Outraged vampires clamored for a law to protect themselves from dhampirs. My very species was considered a threat to society. I was a rabid dog that needed to be put down. A neurotic Queen Britannia was only too happy to placate them.

For years I was plagued by nightmares of Kendall Masters and her uncle. I'd wake up screaming in my mother's comforting arms. Later, after her death, I'd wake up in the tunnels shaking. Kami learned the name Kendall Masters thanks to the number of times I mumbled it in my sleep.

"Now I remember her," Callan said. "She glowed pink."

"Silver," Davina corrected him. "Don't you know anything?"

"Seems like you know quite a lot. Those history lessons must be paying off."

Davina glowered at him. "Don't patronize me, brother."

A vampire poked his head in the doorway and cleared his throat. "Forgive the interruption. Your Highness, it's time for your lesson."

"Very well." She looked at me. "I'll only be an hour. Will you stay until I finish?"

"Sadly not. I have work to do."

"For the banner?" she asked eagerly. "I could join you."

"Not this time," I said.

"Or ever," Callan added. He clapped a hand on Davina's shoulder. "Your parents are fond of Miss Hayes, but they wouldn't take kindly to anyone who put you in harm's way."

"Enjoy your lesson," I said.

"Fat chance," she grumbled.

I passed the instructor and followed Callan out of the study. As long as I had his attention, I figured it was worth inquiring about the travel ban.

"Can we talk somewhere in private?" I asked.

He gestured around the empty corridor. "There's no one around."

I shook my head.

"I see. Follow me then."

He guided me through the cavernous palace rooms to a corridor. I recognized it as the one that connected to a secret tunnel where I'd seen Adwin, the royal winemaker and

Callan's partner-in-crime, carrying bottles of synthetic blood. Callan hadn't seen fit to tell me about his secret experiment, so I hadn't seen fit to inquire about it.

He popped open a door and ushered me inside. A cursory glance revealed we were in the room where Adwin stored the bottles before transferring them to the palace wine cellar.

Callan stood in front of a stack of crates, his expression stony. "I warned you to stay away from me and you show up at the palace?"

I ignored his rebuke. "Did you put me on a restricted list?"

His brow creased. "What do you mean?"

"I applied for a travel pass and found out I've been banned from travel."

"Are you certain?"

"Yes. There were also instructions to alert someone in House Lewis to my application. Is that someone you?"

He dragged a thoughtful hand through his hair. "Of course not. Why would I want to prevent you from traveling?"

I folded my arms. "I don't know. You tell me."

"If you recall, I'm the one who wants you to keep a safe distance."

"Safe? Or just distance?"

He didn't react.

It was foolish of me to care—to think our time in Devon had meant anything to him. He was the Highland Reckoning. The Demon of House Duncan. And I was just...

A dhampir. The natural enemy of full-blooded vampires.

If ever there was a star-crossed couple, it was us.

But Callan didn't know my true nature, which begged

the question—what was he trying to protect me from? I'd initially thought it was Louise, an ambitious princess of House Peyton with her eye on Callan as a suitor. Callan had dispelled me of that notion though.

"I bet the ban is from when you were working for the West End pack. The system hasn't been updated yet, that's all. I'll have a word with Maeron."

The whole reason Callan and I had traveled to Devon together was because Maeron had wanted eyes on me. Callan then decided he'd rather those eyes be his than anyone else's. The thought gave me a rush of pleasure which I quickly dismissed. Clearly his feelings had since dissipated.

"If the alert is old, then why is it a travel ban and not simply a report of my destination? Your brother wanted to track my movements, not stop me from making any."

Callan appeared unconcerned. "Could be a glitch. Mistakes happen, especially when it comes to bureaucracy."

"Could be." Little did he know I'd taken possession of the Transcendence Stone from Romeo prior to his arrest. If Maeron suspected that Romeo had lied about the stone's whereabouts, that would explain his desire to keep me contained. The vampire prince had no idea that I was capable of opening doors to other dimensions. No travel required for hiding stones.

"If you'd like me to speak to him..."

"Please don't."

Callan looked at me quizzically.

"Your brother doesn't seem to like me very much," I said quickly. "I don't want him to think I was complaining about him." And if he was suspicious of me, I really didn't want him to know I was aware.

"Fair enough. If you need to travel, I can help you. You don't need to tell me where."

My eyebrows shot up. "You're not going to ask why?"

"As you said earlier, it isn't my business. You're a knight, Hayes, and your intentions have always been noble. I don't see why I should question your motives."

"Will you tell me why you think you're a danger to me?"

He blew out a breath. "The less you know, the better."

The prince sounded like me, using ignorance as a shield to protect my loved ones. It didn't feel so good now that the shoe was on the other foot.

"Go to Tottenham Stables at midnight. Adwin will meet you there," he continued.

"The royal winemaker wears many hats."

Standing amidst the contraband, I wondered whether Callan might tell me about his secret experiment.

"That he does," Callan replied, disappointing me once again.

Fine. Keep your secrets. I have enough of my own.

"Why not lend me the pass for Ms. Washington?" That was the fake travel pass I'd used to cross the border into Devon with him.

"Because a trip to another territory so close in time to Devon might raise a red flag. Best to be cautious."

That made sense.

Callan angled his head toward the door. "Take the tunnel outside if you don't want anyone to see you."

"What makes you think I don't want to be seen?"

His gaze raked over me. "Aside from the fact that you're dressed like a sexy ninja, I saw your face with Davina. You have no desire to be in the palace. It's obvious you're uncomfortable here."

He had no idea.

"Sexy ninja, huh?"

He exhaled softly. "I knew I shouldn't have said that."

"Thank you, Your Highness. I appreciate your help and the compliment." As I turned toward the door, he latched on to my arm.

"London..."

I looked back at him—a perfect package of precision and power—and hoped I didn't appear as hopeful as I felt. "Yes?"

He released his grip. "Safe travels, wherever you're headed."

I felt torn between slapping him and kissing him—the usual mix of emotions when it came to the Beast of Birmingham.

"Thank you," I said, and slipped away quietly like only a sexy ninja could.

I RETURNED to the flat and called the office to let Minka know I'd be out of commission for a couple days.

"What are you up to?" Minka asked, as direct and nosy as ever.

"What makes you think I'm up to something?"

"You don't have an active job on the docket, you don't have any sick relatives to tend to, and you never take a holiday."

"Consider them mental health days."

Minka sighed into the phone. "You're always so secretive, London."

"I'm not being secretive. I'm being considerate. I'm telling you I won't be around for a couple days so you don't worry."

She snorted. "You're not special. I'm neurotic. I worry about everyone."

There was acknowledging your flaws and then there was Minka.

I hung up the phone and prepared the magic circle that I used to access the pocket dimension where I'd stored the stones as well as the menagerie when circumstances required it. I dubbed the realm their 'holiday home.' It was a place to keep the animals safe while I was away and couldn't care for them. Barnaby was the only one I left to his own devices. The raven was perfectly capable of flying around the city for days without assistance from me.

I gathered the animals and sent them through the portal. I warned Hera not to be too vigorous with the scratching post where I'd hidden the Elemental Stone along with the Transcendence Stone. They were currently covered in a layer of hideous green carpet where no one would ever find them.

I changed into my magical armor and loaded myself with the usual weapons. I strapped Babe to my back and tucked my daggers, affectionately known as Bert and Ernie, out of sight.

I took a bus north to Tottenham Stables. I had a hard time believing Callan had arranged for me to ride a horse all the way to Wales. Maybe there was a car hidden in the stables for emergency use. Preferably a fast one. My driving skills were limited, but I'd manage if forced.

Upon arrival it was clear these weren't the official royal stables. The only evidence the stables even existed was a worn wooden sign that hung crooked from a fencepost.

A familiar figure stepped from the darkness as though chiseled from a block of pure black.

I smiled at the royal winemaker. "Nice to see you again, Adwin."

He inclined his head in greeting. "The luxury of friends in high places."

"I really appreciate your help."

"Save your appreciation for the prince. He's the one making the arrangements."

Quietly, I hoped.

Adwin crooked a finger. "You're in for a special treat."

I followed him to a stable door, which he opened with a flourish. My mode of transport wasn't a horse or a car.

A white winged horse whinnied at the sight of us.

"A pegasus," I said in awe.

"I told you."

"She's a beauty." Where did Callan acquire a domestic pegasus? Who was I kidding? The vampire prince had assets and resources I couldn't even dream of.

Adwin walked over and stroked the creature's head. "I haven't had the pleasure of riding her myself. Perhaps someday."

A man emerged from the shadows and ambled toward us. His brown hair was unkempt and he wore overalls with a crumpled blue shirt underneath. "This her?"

"Ms. Washington, yes," Adwin replied. "Ms. Washington, this is Arthur."

"A pleasure to meet you," I said.

Arthur spat on the ground. "This is Mimsy. She's been fed and watered."

"And saddled and bridled, I see."

"Figured you might need the extra support. You take good care of her or I'll hunt you down like a rare red woodpecker."

I frowned. "You would hunt a rare bird?"

"Not to kill. Just to admire it."

"It's Arthur's charming way of warning you to look after Mimsy." Adwin inclined his head toward the pegasus.

"I have no plans to endanger her." I joined Adwin in stroking her. "You are gorgeous."

She whinnied softly in response.

"Well, she seems to like you," Arthur said. "That counts for something. When do you expect to have her back?"

"I'm not sure. Twenty-four hours, give or take."

He nodded. "I'll be here."

"Any special instructions?" I asked.

Arthur shrugged. "She likes carrots. Oh, and don't fall off and die."

"I've ridden dragons. I should be able to manage a horse with wings."

Arthur left the stable with a grunt.

"He's rough around the edges," Adwin said, "but he takes glorious care of the animals."

"That's all that matters." I approached the pegasus.

"Mimsy will get you across the border safely and secretly. She's designed for stealth."

I didn't ask for details, not that I'd get them. "Thank you, Adwin."

"You can thank Prince Callan in person when you've returned safely."

"He's avoiding me," I admitted. It was pointless to share this development with the winemaker, but he obviously knew the prince well. Maybe he knew more than Callan was willing to divulge.

Adwin gave me a sympathetic look. "I can't pretend to know his reasons, but I can tell you that he wouldn't go to the trouble of helping you if he didn't care about you." He backed away from the pegasus. "Bon voyage, Miss Hayes."

Deadly Knight   41

Mimsy was taller than she looked. I used a stool to climb onto the saddle, dodging a wide wing as it flapped toward me. Adwin cleared a path and the pegasus charged out of the stable. I tightened my hold on the bridle as she picked up speed. Cold wind blasted my exposed skin and I shivered as Mimsy spread her wings wide and flew.

I'd never been to Wales—never had the need or desire to travel there. Wales was the territory of House Kane. Relations between the Houses were relatively peaceful, which made flying into their airspace a little less nauseating. Still, I was grateful for whatever magical mojo Mimsy was sporting to remain undetected.

I let Mimsy choose her preferred course. The pegasus seemed to know what she was doing so I clung to her and enjoyed the ride. Once outside the city, it was difficult to see the land below through the haze of darkness, but I could make out the silhouette of undulating hills. I'd seen enough old photographs of the countryside to know what they looked like in sunlight. The people who lived back then didn't know how fortunate they were. Blue skies. Daylight. Vampires still relegated to the shadows. It was hard to imagine such a world had ever existed.

A waterway became visible on the horizon and I recognized the shape of the Bristol Channel. My mother's geography lessons had once again proven useful. As soon as we made it past the channel, we'd be in House Kane territory.

I held my breath as we crossed the aerial border and only released it when I was certain we'd made it safely. I steered the pegasus north toward Snowdon, the highest mountain in Wales. Snowdon was the highest point in the British Isles, except for the Scottish Highlands—another place I'd yet to see. The mountain had been formed by rocks generated by volcanoes during the Ordovician period. If those volcanoes had been part of the Great Eruption, there was every chance the British Isles would've gone the way of South America. The stones and their magical secrets would likely have been lost forever.

As we flew closer to the mountain, magic started to press against me from all sides. I couldn't see anything through the thick clouds. The Atheneum had to be getting close. Nothing else in the region was infused with the kind of intense power I felt.

Mimsy bucked, appearing to sense the magic too. I stroked her mane and whispered soothing words in her ear. If she overreacted, I'd seize her mind, but I preferred to avoid it unless it was absolutely necessary. I respected my ability as well as the animals whose minds I poked and prodded.

Finally the clouds parted, revealing an enormous marble wall and the Atheneum beyond. An involuntary gasp escaped me. What would my mother say if she could see me now?

I calmed Mimsy and directed her to land.

Knowledge was about to be served to me on a platter and I was very, very hungry.

4

The terrain was unsurprisingly rocky, but there were plenty of flat areas to land. The mountain had been sculpted first by nature and later by the builders of the Atheneum. No one knew for certain who was responsible for this repository of knowledge. Some claimed that dwarfs were responsible, while others suggested that dwarfs had merely performed the labor assigned to them by a coven of witches. No group had ever directly taken credit for the institution. Even House Kent admitted ignorance despite the Atheneum's presence in their territory.

The building's rounded style reminded me of pictures I'd seen of the Colosseum except the Atheneum sported a dome. An enormous marble wall blocked my path. From my vantage point, the barrier appeared to wrap all the way around the mountainside although I had a hard time believing it. Then again, I'd seen pictures of the Great Wall of China. I approached the wall in search of a latch or other mechanism and placed my palm flat on the cool surface. If there was an official entrance, I didn't see any evidence of it.

Behind me Mimsy let loose a distressed whinny.

"It's okay," I said in a soothing tone. "It's only a fancy library. Nothing will hurt you."

The pegasus backed away, seemingly unconvinced.

A white tiger chose that particular moment to make a liar out of me. He peeled himself away from the white wall —all six feet of him. His paws were larger than my head and his ice blue eyes regarded me coolly as he padded forward.

Mimsy didn't wait for instructions. She spread her wings and fled the mountainside. I couldn't blame her. I was terrified too. But I had to stay. The desire for what was beyond the wall was stronger than my fear.

"Who here requests entry to the Atheneum?" the tiger thundered.

My heart pounded. "London Hayes, Knight of Boudica."

"Boudica," he echoed. "Now there was a great warrior. You seek knowledge on behalf of your banner?"

It seemed unwise to lie to a creature that could easily bite off my head and use my body to pick the hair from his fangs afterward. "I seek knowledge on behalf of everyone."

Another slab of the marble wall trembled. A white dragon tore its wings from the marble gate and the rest of its body followed. Its pearlescent scales glinted in the darkness. I'd never seen a dragon like this one.

"You have a connection to us," the dragon said. Her soft, melodic voice was in sharp contrast to the thunderous voice of the tiger.

"I have a connection to most animals."

The tiger cocked his head. "Is that so? Do you know my name?"

I concentrated on the tiger's blue eyes and tried to solidify the connection without actually penetrating his mind. A single word flashed in my mind.

"Quinn."

The tiger bowed his head in acknowledgement.

I switched my focus to the dragon. "Liya."

The tiger and dragon exchanged glances.

"What do people usually guess? Merlin and Morgana? Anthony and Cleopatra?"

"You must prove your worthiness to enter these walls," the dragon said, ignoring me.

"At home I only need a library card."

"This is no ordinary library," Quinn said.

"So guessing your names isn't enough to show I'm worthy?" I didn't think it would be that simple, but a girl could dream.

"You must pass a test," Quinn said.

My skin began to tingle. I turned around but saw nothing but empty mountain behind me. "Before we get started, can you just tell me whether there are any vampires around?"

"Two," Liya replied. "They've parked a vehicle a mile down the mountain and are approaching on foot."

"How did you know that?" the tiger asked.

"You have your special brand of knowledge and I have mine," I told them.

The tingling sensation intensified and I pivoted to confront the two vampires as they came into view. One was blond and stocky and the other was red-haired and cordoned with muscle.

"I take it they're not guardians like you," I said.

"No. They are visitors like you," Liya said.

I resisted the urge to produce a weapon. Maybe their arrival was a coincidence. Unlikely but worth exploring before we came to blows. I didn't want to end up in a House Kane dungeon. It was bad enough my ride had abandoned me. I'd cross that bridge home when I came to it though.

"Pardon me, gentlemen, but you'll have to wait your turn," I told the vampires.

"There's a test," I said. "And that means I need complete privacy or else I'll have performance anxiety."

The stocky vampire took a step forward. His hair was cut short on the sides and back but longer at the top. His cherubic face made him look much younger than he probably was, though it was often hard to tell a vampire's age. Unless they had silver in their hair, it was anyone's guess.

"We'll pass that test then," he said. "No performance anxiety here."

"I think your girlfriend might tell a different story."

The redhead's effusive laughter quickly morphed into a cough.

"What information are you looking for? Maybe I can help while I'm in there." I jabbed a thumb in the direction of the building.

The redhead folded his arms, muscles bulging, and smirked. "Friseal's Temple."

The stocky blonde elbowed his companion in the ribs. "We're not supposed to tell anyone, remember?"

"We can tell her," the redhead said. "She won't talk."

"She seems to be doing a good job of it right now."

The redhead's mouth split into a grin. "Maybe so, but the dead don't speak now, do they?"

"Well, she ain't dead yet," the blonde said.

"Who sent you?" I asked. And whoever it was, why did they choose to send two buffoons without the brain power between them to change a lightbulb?

"Our boss wishes to remain anonymous," the blonde said.

"Did you follow me?" And if they did, how? According to Adwin, there was no way they could've tracked Mimsy.

"Why would we follow a random witch?" The redhead cracked his knuckles. "Now, out of our way. The boss is waiting for answers and I guarantee he's more important than whoever you're working for."

"What makes you think I work for anyone?"

The redhead motioned to my outfit. "That get-up for starters."

I wondered whether their boss was the same one who'd confiscated the pages from the library. If so, it meant the pages didn't include sufficient information about the temple. Whatever happened next, I couldn't let them inside the Atheneum.

I whipped back toward the guardians. "Test me. I'm ready."

A strong hand clamped down on my shoulder and jerked me off my feet.

"Fine. Have it your way." I'd fight first. Test later.

The blonde snickered. "We usually do."

I rolled to my feet and produced my axe. "I'd like to introduce you to a good friend of mine called Babe." I swung the blade and nicked the blonde's arm as he turned away. He was faster than his stocky body suggested.

"We're vampires not trees," the redhead said. "Do you really think your little axe will be enough?"

I flicked my wrist left to right. "What makes you think Babe's the only tool in my box?" I lunged at the blonde, kicking out my back foot to block the redhead's attack. He staggered backward, appearing surprised by my quick reaction.

The blonde gripped my wrist and twisted my arm behind my back. "Even if you get in, we'll just wait for you to come out and torture you later."

I clucked my tongue. "Promises, promises."

I whipped my head back and smashed it against the vampire's nose. I broke free of his grip and spun around to face them.

The blonde rubbed his bloody nose. "You'll regret that."

"Doubtful." I whipped the axe from side to side to limber up my wrists.

The redhead sprang forward and I blocked his assault with a blast of air that blew him backward like a wayward leaf. Elemental magic wasn't my strong suit, but it would do in a pinch.

Once again the blond vampire's speed took me by surprise. He grabbed my hair and yanked me toward him. I raised the axe and sliced the blade straight down, separating his arm from the rest of his body. A clump of my hair was still clutched in his severed hand. Staring at the empty shoulder socket, the vampire slumped to the ground.

The redhead marched toward me with a menacing glint in his eye. "You'll pay for that."

"He isn't dead, only maimed." Vampires were blessed with impressive healing abilities. Helped with the whole immortality thing.

On the ground his companion howled in agony.

The redhead seemed torn between helping his companion and hurting me.

"What's your plan?" I pressed. "This is House Kane territory. How do you think the king and queen will feel when two vampires show up on their doorstep to complain about a knight?"

"I'm planning to kill you, not complain about you." The redhead's companion whimpered, drawing his attention to the ground. "Ah, hell."

I produced a cloth and made a show of cleaning the

blonde's blood from the blade. Anything to dissuade the redhead from further action.

Wordlessly he lifted his companion over his shoulder and staggered under the weight.

"What are you going to tell your boss?" I asked out of curiosity. Thugs like these two generally didn't want to admit they'd been beaten by a woman.

"We were ambushed by the Mierce."

I regarded him. "You were awfully quick with that answer."

"We passed by one of their caravans on the way here. Seems like a plausible explanation." He started to carry his friend down the mountainside. "I'll be back for the arm," he called over his shoulder.

I held up my hands. "Wouldn't dream of touching it." I turned to face the guardians. I hoped they weren't so disgusted by my performance that they withdrew their offer of a test.

"You may enter," the white tiger said, shocking the hell out of me.

"But I haven't been tested yet." I flicked a glance over my shoulder at the vampires. "It can't be those two. It's not like you sent them to attack me."

"The test is not set in stone," Liya said.

"You've proven your worth," Quinn added.

"Because I ripped off a vampire's arm?" That didn't prove I was worthy. It only proved that I was violent when necessary.

"The fight itself is not the test," Quinn said. "You could've easily killed them both, yet you chose to let them live."

"It could've gone either way," I lied. Truth be told I could've killed them both in ten seconds flat.

A low growl emanated from the tiger. "Would you like to enter or not?"

It seemed unwise to stand around arguing with my victory. Uncertain what to do next, I bowed. "Thank you."

"We hope you find the knowledge you seek." The white tiger retreated to the marble and the dragon followed suit. Once they were camouflaged by the wall, a doorway slid aside to admit me.

I glanced in the direction of the vampires, wondering if the redhead would attempt to slip in behind me. If so, I had a feeling he wouldn't get too far. He might even find himself with a missing limb to match his friend if the guardians decided to close the doorway at the wrong time.

Or the right time.

The sound of a truck motor in the distance reassured me that the vampires were abandoning their mission. Good. I'd worry about my own transportation later. Right now there was a more important task to complete.

I passed through the gap and heard the slab of marble shift closed behind me. I took a moment to sheath the axe. I didn't get the sense there'd be any obstacles inside.

I approached the arched double doors and they creaked open in greeting. Magic pulsed as I crossed the threshold into the atrium where seven circular levels surrounded me. I blinked twice to make sure there was nothing wrong with my vision. There was nary a book in sight. In place of stacks of dusty tomes were seemingly endless shelves lined with colorful potion bottles. Shades of blue, red, green, and yellow danced against the plain walls. The sole source of light appeared to be from the bottles themselves. I saw no sign of electricity.

A crick formed in my neck from holding it at an uncomfortable angle and I stretched from side to side.

Where to even begin?

I hunted for an indexing system, a set of instructions—anything to tell me how to find the information on Friseal's Temple. I surveyed the first set of shelves and noticed small labels with indecipherable symbols. If they were written in a language I didn't understand, that presented an additional problem. I touched the nearest label and observed the symbols reform into recognizable letters. 'Physics' was written in English.

So much for the dwarf theory. No way did dwarfs create this place. They didn't possess the necessary skills. Labor, yes. Magic, not a chance. I couldn't fathom the immense power necessary to sustain this place. Layers of magic woven together to form the patchwork of knowledge. I had no doubt each label was translatable into the visitor's native language. Presumably if I wanted to learn about physics, I'd drink the potion and the bottle would refill for the next seeker of knowledge. Did it tell me everything there was to know about physics? That seemed awfully broad. Maybe I was meant to ask a question or make a specific request.

I looked around the room. There had to be a card catalogue somewhere. I could easily spend a lifetime in this building drinking and learning if I couldn't narrow the scope. Too bad the Atheneum didn't have its own Pedro.

I wandered through an arched doorway and into the next room where the shelves were lined with unlit white candles. What was the difference between potions and candles?

I paused in front of a sign and touched the unfamiliar symbols. *Light a candle and all will be revealed.*

All? That was a pretty big promise. I touched another label and watched the symbols reform into English—*King Charles I*.

Did the Atheneum have information about the former monarch that wasn't included in the history books? Or was this simply an additional resource?

I wondered whether the candles were only for key figures. There didn't seem to be enough to include the entire population. If there was a candle here harboring my secret, I had a hard time believing anyone would ever find it or care enough to light it. Still, the possibility worried me. Queen Britannia wasn't the only one to suffer from paranoia it seemed.

Not wanting to lose focus, I returned to the main atrium and debated the potion bottles. I was granted permission to enter. What now? Maybe it was a multi-pronged approach and I had to prove something else to gain access to the actual information. That seemed unlikely and unnecessarily complicated. Then again, if someone like Minka was in charge of creating this place, it was plausible.

"I seek information on Friseal's Temple," I announced to the empty air.

The sound of rustling drew my attention upward. I watched for any sign of movement. A white bird emerged from the top level and flew toward me. At first glance I thought it was a type of a seabird.

Not a seabird.

An albino raven.

The bird flew toward me with a potion bottle clutched in its claws. Once it was within reach, it released the bottle into my cupped hands. The bottle was surprisingly light and filled with a blue and yellow liquid that somehow managed to retain their individual properties rather than appear green.

"Thank you."

The raven cawed and flew away. I had to imagine Pedro would be pretty upset if he lost his job to a bird.

I popped a cork from the bottle and sniffed. The scent of basil overpowered my nostrils. At least I liked the smell of basil. I could think of worse scents.

I gulped down the thick liquid. It tasted like a smoothie that combined so many ingredients that you couldn't identify a single one. Ironically I didn't even taste basil. If tastes were colors, this one was green without question.

My head swam with images and I felt overcome by dizziness.

Don't vomit.

I fought the wave of nausea and focused on slowing the images in my mind. At the very least it would help with the dizziness. Eventually the parade of images slowed to a standstill until there was only one. It featured a row of different species—among them were vampires, witches and wizards, dwarfs, humans, and werewolves. There was another one I believed to be a myth, even now.

Fae.

With slightly pointed ears and a long, narrow face with glowing silver skin, there was no mistaking her for another species.

I glanced at my own arms and contemplated the glow. Could I be descended from a fae bloodline? No, that didn't make sense. My mother was a witch and my father was a vampire. The silver glow was a telltale sign of my dhampir biology. Nothing to do with fae. Still, the silver glow was intriguing.

I tried my best to absorb the details as the information washed over me. Some information was readily apparent like the fact that vampires and werewolves remained insular throughout the centuries. Fae began procreating with humans, witches, and wizards to the point where they ceased to exist as an independent species. In Devon I'd met a man who boasted of fae in his bloodline. I'd dismissed his claim as a bedtime story invented to make a boy feel special.

Consider me schooled.

My head snapped back as the row of species morphed into another scene. The same figures formed a circle along with additional members of their species, except for humans and dwarfs. Each group poured their magic into stones. A wizard directed their actions. His face was as plain and indistinguishable as his brown cloak. Friseal, I presumed. Stone by stone, they built a temple that reached toward the heavens. Similar to the Great Pyramid of Cholula that Antonia Birch had described, these supernatural species combined their magic and created a tower in an attempt to reach the heavens. Then the sky darkened and crackled with lightning. The creatures cowered in response to the angry gods. The tower was obliterated and the pieces scattered.

As the stones broke apart and were absorbed by the earth, the temple's destruction yielded an unexpected result. Red, blue, yellow, and green. The colors flashed in the air until they merged together to form a black hole. A powerful type of magic emanated from the circle. I felt its presence as though we weren't separated by time and space.

No, it couldn't be.

When the stones were destroyed, it appeared that their powers co-mingled and created a new type of magic. A type of magic that was usually mentioned in hushed tones or brushed off entirely.

Chaos magic.

Like the existence of fae, I believed chaos magic was nothing more than a myth. Until now.

When the supervolcanoes erupted, they pushed long-buried secrets from the center of the earth to the surface once again. They spewed ash into the atmosphere along with forgotten monsters.

And forgotten stones.

Five stones hovered in my mind's eye.

Of the many stones used to build the temple, only five had survived. Three I recognized. I was a ghost among them, a silent observer of time. Their images were magnified as though the universe wanted me to be certain my eyes didn't deceive me. Knowledge in 3-D.

I tried to make sense of the vision. The Great Eruption happened after the construction of Albemarle in Devon where the Transcendence Stone had been discovered as part of the crumbling wall of an estate. Meanwhile vampires had maintained control of the Immortality Stone for centuries. So how could the Great Eruption be the reason for the stones resurfacing? Timeline aside, not one of the ten supervolcanoes that erupted were in this part of the world.

I studied the image of the stones. My mother taught me that life is a cycle and history repeats itself. What if there'd been another Great Eruption long ago before recorded history? It was possible that a much earlier eruption spit the stones back to the earth's surface where they remained buried for centuries. The remnants of Friseal's Temple had been resting quietly and awaiting our discovery.

My thoughts returned to the fae's silver glow. Until this moment, I'd believed my magic was unstable and unpredictable because of my dhampir blood.

What if I was wrong?

Like most of the population, I'd scoffed at the notion of chaos magic and fae, even while being accepting of new ideas. We all had blind spots, apparently, even those of us who prided ourselves on our open-mindedness.

It seemed my abilities weren't as clear-cut as I'd previously believed. If my interpretation of the vision was correct, they stemmed from a heritage much older than my mother and her vampire consort. They came from chaos magic. I'd inherited remnants of all the magic that existed in the universe. It explained so much.

And yielded so many new questions.

"Where are the remaining two stones?" I asked.

The image of the stones dissipated, leaving only an inky void. Maybe the Atheneum didn't know the answer to every question. I had to try another tack.

It occurred to me if I could identify the original location of the temple, I could see whether the remaining two stones were there. Just like this very mountain had been formed by an old volcano, it was possible the site of the temple had been built on one too. One that later exploded and spilled its secrets.

"Where was Friseal's Temple built?"

In response, a sandstone cliff rose into view. As I inhaled the salty air, nausea seized hold of me. I dropped to my knees on the hard floor and clutched my stomach. The images kept coming but I failed to register them. An invisible drum started to pound inside my head. The nausea and discomfort became too overwhelming and I released the connection. The images came to an abrupt stop. My eyes blinked open and I noticed the bright silver glow of my skin. No wonder I'd started to feel sick. I'd been so intent on the visions that I neglected to notice my system was ready to burst.

I shifted to my side and focused on regulating my breathing. That helped with the nausea. I pushed through the headache and connected to my magic. Opening my palm flat, I released a blast of air. Not enough air to topple over any potion bottles but enough to offer me relief.

The silver faded but remained visible, dots of light shining through my skin like a constellation. I needed to use more.

"Levitas," I said. My body lifted and hovered above the gleaming marble floor.

My skin returned to its usual shade of pale and I struggled to my feet. This experience gave a whole new meaning to the term 'book hangover.'

I looked around for the potion bottle to see whether I could try again, but there was no sign of it. I'd have to try to piece together what I could remember.

As I pivoted toward the exit, the candle room caught my eye. So many skeletons in one small closet. The history buff in me felt drawn to explore the options. Then again, knowing the truth about someone like Charles I or Henry VIII wouldn't change history.

Except not all royal secrets were too distant to matter.

My palms began to itch with anticipation. This was my chance to answer a question without an official answer on record—whether the two warring kings of Houses Lewis and Duncan had conspired to murder Queen Britannia. It wouldn't change the past, but it could change the future. Davina and Callan deserved to know the truth. Even obnoxious Maeron deserved to know whether his father was complicit in the murder of his mother. I was already here. What harm could it do?

I crossed the threshold into the candle room. Each white candle was identical in appearance. At least I knew how the system worked now.

"King Casek," I announced. I could've chosen King

Glendon, but I was more interested in seeing the truth from the husband's point of view. King Glendon's reasons were obvious. Casek's were less so, assuming the rumors were even true. Maybe the candle would absolve the head of House Lewis of any wrongdoing in connection with his wife's death and I'd have nothing to tell.

I glanced toward the ceiling for the albino raven. Instead a candle at eye level slid forward across the shelf. I crossed the room and touched the label. Sure enough, the symbols reformed into *King Casek of House Lewis*.

My gaze swept the shelves for a match. I found a long stick and scraped it against the base of the candlestick, producing a flame. I lit the wick and a vision of a familiar face flooded my vision. King Casek smiled, his fangs gleaming in the dim light. His gray eyes were as kindly as ever. Was this truly the face of someone willing to conspire with the enemy and murder his wife?

It occurred to me that I should've asked a specific question. I didn't want his life's story. Casek was a vampire. I didn't have that kind of time. Before I could open my mouth to narrow the scope of the request, another image appeared —one that sent me spiraling.

Her face looked exactly the way I remembered it. Lively, intelligent eyes and an endearingly crooked mouth that promised knowledge as well as comfort. And laughter. Always laughter.

Rhea Hayes. My mother.

I stumbled backward and nearly dropped the candle. Was this some kind of trick? An illusion?

No. The Atheneum contained only facts. My mother was in this vision for a reason. I steadied my breathing and allowed the images to unfold.

She entered the palace. The hem of her dress swished

around her calves. It was a plain dress that I didn't remember—cobalt blue with a black lace collar. A lump formed in my throat. Gods, she was beautiful. My bones ached from missing her so much.

The image flashed to a classroom. I gasped in recognition of Davina's study. I watched as my mother demonstrated magic to a half dozen eager vampire children. I remembered the children of staff were included in the lessons then. King Casek lingered in the doorway. He couldn't see me, of course, but he wouldn't have noticed me anyway. His gaze was firmly fixed on my mother. They locked eyes and she smiled. His body went rigid but his cheeks flushed with the pleasure of being singled out by her.

The images swirled and colors shifted. I was in a different room now, one I didn't recognize. It wasn't the palace. The ceiling was too low and the furnishings too dull. I recognized a blanket draped over the chair as one my mother had knitted by hand. This must've been her home before I was born.

Casek cupped her cheeks in his hands. Although I couldn't hear the words they exchanged, it was clear from the way they looked at each other that they were in love. I'd never seen my mother dreamy-eyed. The only time she'd ever looked remotely wistful was when she described her brief time at the palace. At the time her sentimentality had surprised me. It was so unlike the sharp, no-nonsense woman I knew.

Now it made sense. It was the place where she'd met the love of her life. It was the home where he still lived. No wonder she'd gone into hiding when she discovered she was pregnant. Giving birth to a dhampir was bad enough, but giving birth to the child of a vampire king...Queen Britannia's husband.

I felt a pang of guilt. If not for me, maybe they'd still be together. She'd chosen me over him.

Then again, Britannia would've torn my mother limb from limb if she'd discovered the affair. Maybe it was for the best that my mother fled with me. I'd added years to her life.

Had Casek killed Britannia in order to pursue a relationship with my mother?

No. That was unlikely. A marriage to a common witch like my mother would've spawned a revolution. Casek was neither strong enough nor foolish enough to travel that path. He wouldn't have killed the most powerful vampire in the land for Rhea Hayes. My mother had been right to leave.

Did he miss her as much as I did? Did he search for her after Britannia's death or was Imogen already selected as his next bride? The current queen had been a strategic choice, after all. A union between Houses. My mother couldn't have offered him that.

I choked back tears as he kissed each cheek and then her patient lips. There was a surprising tenderness between them that made me ache with longing for the comfort of my mother's arms.

The next image was Casek entering the same room and finding it empty. He tore the place apart, lifting furniture as though he might find my mother curled up beneath the sofa and waiting to surprise him. He punched the door straight off the hinges and marched out.

The images dissipated and I was back in the candle room at the Atheneum. This wasn't the information I'd intended to uncover, but the Atheneum clearly had other plans for me.

No one could ever know.

I used the flame to burn the label so no one would know

which figure's information had been destroyed. Then I blew out the candle, plucked out the wick, and snapped the candlestick in half. I wasn't proud of my actions—I was raised to believe knowledge was sacrosanct—but I had to protect myself.

The floor rumbled its displeasure.

"I'm sorry," I called to no one in particular. "I couldn't take the chance."

A low voice rumbled. "Banned," it hissed. "Forever."

A cold gust of wind wrapped around me like a straitjacket and lifted me into the air. I fought against its tight embrace to no avail. It carried me out of the candle room, through the atrium, and ejected me from the building. I landed on my backside as the double doors slammed shut behind me.

I remained flat on the ground, my axe digging into my back, and stared at the dark canopy above my head as I tried to come to terms with the revelation.

I raised my chin to the heavens and whispered in disbelief, "King Casek is my father."

5

I trudged down the mountainside in search of transportation. If the vampires were right about a caravan of Mierce, I might be able to hitch a ride part of the way. I'd encountered them in Devon too. Although my interaction with the humans hadn't been pleasant, it was possible this group would be less likely to try and sacrifice me to the gods.

I tried to focus on the route rather than the information I'd acquired. My efforts, however, were in vain.

I am the daughter of King Casek.

I am a princess.

Davina was my half-sister.

Good grief. Maeron was my half-brother.

None of that mattered when it came to my fate. The law didn't care whether my blood was royal. If anything, that made me even more dangerous in the eyes of vampires. They'd assume my unusual powers were inherited from the king rather than the generations of supernaturals that came before us.

My skin began to prick. Terrific. Maybe the two vampires

decided to stick around after all. I wasn't in the mood to fight.

I peered into the gloaming ahead. A lone figure strode toward me. His broad shoulders cut through the murky mist. His green eyes stood out like two blades of grass amongst a field of ash.

"You have a strange definition of keeping your distance," I told Callan.

He continued to advance toward me. "I thought Wales was a safe bet."

"Safe from what?"

He didn't answer as he halted directly in my path.

"How did you know where to find me?"

"The pegasus, of course."

She must've worn a tracker. "Why are you here?"

He cocked his head and looked at me with an expression bordering on affection. "Mimsy returned to the stables without you. Naturally I was concerned."

"I'm a knight, Your Royal Worrywart. I can find my way back without help."

"I wasn't worried you were lost. I was worried..." His face darkened. "Never mind."

"You don't need to worry about me, but as long as you're here, you might as well help me get home."

He rocked back and forth on his heels. "No worries. As soon as I find us a vehicle, we'll be on our way."

"You don't have a vehicle? Did you ride Mimsy?"

"No, she refused to leave the stables. Something spooked her which is why I was so concerned."

"Then how did you get here so quickly?" I asked.

He frowned. "Quickly? It seemed to take forever. First there was a car out of the city. They traveled as far as Oxford. Then a very nice lady picked me up in a vintage

Jaguar. I crossed the border in the back of a van under a pile of rugs. They were none the wiser. I rode in the back of a flatbed until I reached Snowdonia and voila." He extended his arms.

"You snuck across the border like a common criminal? Look at you, Mr. Lawbreaker."

"It seemed necessary at the time." His gaze traveled over me. "Now that I can see you're in good shape and spirits, I'm having second thoughts about my decision."

"Ha! Too late." I scratched the back of my head. "I must've been in the Atheneum for longer than I realized."

"Time moves differently there. Didn't anybody warn you?"

"No." There were many things nobody bothered to warn me about, including the information that might be revealed.

Callan clapped his hands together. "Let's acquire a new vehicle, shall we?"

"I didn't bring money."

"Good thing I have the funds to cover it."

I feigned surprise. "You have money? Shocker."

He offered a half smile. "I've missed you."

"I saw you at the palace."

"I know, but our meeting was brief."

My mouth formed a thin line. "Not my decision."

"No, but it was my decision to come here to retrieve you safely. Did you get what you came for?"

There was no way I could tell him the truth. "Ask me later when I've been plied with alcohol."

His brow lifted. "Do we have plans at a pub?"

"We do now." I hooked my arm through his. "I'm starving. Buy me supper and then we'll find our mechanical steed to take us home."

The pub at the base of the mountain was called the

Dancing Dragon. It was larger than The Crown but not nearly as nice. The seating was comprised of hard, wooden benches and the ale tasted bitter.

"Do dragons actually dance?" he asked.

We'd opted to split a pitcher and I devoured a plate of couscous and root vegetables. Callan skipped the food, referring to the menu as "unappealing."

I ran the cloth napkin over my mouth in an effort to restore whatever dignity I'd lost inhaling my meal. I probably resembled a black hole sucking in space particles. "Why ask me? How would I know?"

"You've just been to the Atheneum. I thought you were supposed to be wiser when you left."

"Not about the dance moves of dragons."

"More's the pity."

I slapped my hands on the table. "Ready to go?"

"I was lured here under the pretense of learning whether you got what you came for."

"You didn't ply me enough."

He raised his hand to signal to the bartender. "Easily remedied."

I reached across the table and forced his hand to the table. "No more ale. It isn't very good."

His mouth twitched. "I'm glad I'm not the only one who thinks that."

"We can have another drink when we're back in Britannia City." I paused. "Or is that still off limits?"

His expression soured. "Still unwise, I'm afraid."

"More's the pity," I said in a slightly mocking tone. I pulled myself to my feet. "Let's get moving. The car's not going to rent itself."

Callan begrudgingly vacated the table and sauntered to the counter. "We'd like our bill, please."

The bartender peered at him. "I know you."

"Do you?" Callan stiffened.

I knew what he was thinking. If the bartender recognized him, he could end up having an issue with House Kane.

"Sure I do," the bartender said. "You're the Umbridge boy all grown up." He wagged a finger. "Caught you with your hand in the biscuit tin more times than I can count."

Callan smiled. "Sounds like me. Never could get enough biscuits."

The bartender's grin broadened. "Say hello to your family for me, would you? They must be chuffed to have you back in town."

"They certainly are." Callan leaned forward. "As it happens, my friend and I are in need of a vehicle during our stay. Any recommendations?"

The bartender polished a butter knife with a white cloth. "There's a place about two miles south of here. Can't miss it."

"Thanks." Callan paid the bill and we left the pub.

"That poor Umbridge boy," I murmured.

Callan cut a sideways glance at me. "What makes you say that?"

"The rumor will spread that he's grown up to be so handsome with such great taste in women. The real Umbridge boy can't possibly compete."

He chuckled. "Great taste in women, huh?"

I offered a modest shrug as we walked along the dark road. The only illumination was provided by passing headlights.

Callan nudged me with his arm. "I have to give you credit, Hayes. You certainly have a way of making my life more adventurous. Before you came along it was all masquerade balls and ribbon-cutting ceremonies."

"Don't tell Davina. She'll be jealous." I swallowed hard. My sister, Davina. I was still trying to wrap my head around that one.

"It'll be our little secret."

"Speaking of secrets…"

He put a finger to his lips. "We're not speaking of them. That's what makes them secrets."

I ignored him. We were stuck in Wales with no way home and I had liquid courage. Now seemed like a good opportunity to press him for answers and I was seizing it with both hands.

"What threat makes it unsafe for us to see each other in the city, but makes it perfectly acceptable for you to be seen with me in Wales?"

He motioned to the darkness around us. "No one's seeing us in Wales."

I hooked a thumb over my shoulder. "Pretty sure all those people in the pub had working eyesight."

He flashed a mischievous grin. "And all they saw was the Umbridge boy all grown up."

"You got lucky, Callan. Face it, you're a very recognizable figure."

He closed his eyes for a fleeting moment. "I wish I could tell you, but I can't."

"You don't trust me." I kept my gaze on the path ahead, partly to not trip and fall and partly to avoid seeing his face.

"It isn't about whether I trust you." He slowed his pace. "I think we're here."

A squat building sat back from the road. It looked like it had been chiseled out of a single hunk of concrete. 'Cars' was hand-painted in red on a sign. A lone tractor sat on the ground outside.

I motioned to the tractor. "That's called false advertising."

"If it gets us back to Britannia City, it'll be worth it."

"Where am I supposed to hide on a tractor? We still have to cross the border, remember?"

"Yes, but we're returning to House Lewis territory. Much easier when you're with me."

I grunted. "You didn't sing that song in Devon."

"Only because we wanted to keep our journey off the record. You've done what you need to do in Wales. Presumably it doesn't matter now."

Callan didn't wait for my reply. He sauntered through the double doors and I quickly followed. The counter was empty. The sound of static drew my attention to the floor where a woman sat on a striped beach chair with a radio on her lap. With a head covered in a layer of orange frizz and a green pantsuit, she resembled a giant flower.

"Hey, company. Brilliant." She set the radio on the floor beside the chair and struggled to get back on her feet. She thrust a hand toward us. "Help an old lady up, would you? It's like trying to climb out of the womb fully formed."

Callan helped her to a standing position.

"Much obliged," she said. "That's a nice grip you've got there. You work out?"

Callan bared his fangs. "Not really."

She nodded. "Got it. What brings you in here?"

"We need to get to Britannia City," I said. "The bartender at the Dancing Dragon said you could sell us a car."

"Sure, I'll sell you one. The name's Hannah, by the way."

"I'm Mr. Lincoln and this is Ms. Washington."

Hannah's smile widened. "Oh, right. A clandestine affair.

Love those. I once sold an old Bentley to a Mr. and Mrs. Smith. I'm pretty sure Mr. Smith was making a getaway from the actual Mrs. Smith."

"If that were the case, wouldn't I have introduced us as Mr. and Mrs. Washington?" Callan asked.

Hannah ignored his logic. "I always wanted to lose myself in a haze of lust. I've had it on my bucket list, just never encountered the right person. There was one guy I thought it might happen with, but I couldn't get past his name."

"What was it?" I asked.

"Sigmund." She gave me a hard look. "There was no way I was calling that out in ecstasy. It would've taken me right out of the moment every time."

"Well, our relationship is strictly professional," I said. "No ecstasy involved."

She laughed. "Sure, honey."

"I didn't notice any cars outside," I said in an effort to redirect the conversation to the task at hand.

"There are a couple in the back." She ambled to the counter where she swiped a set of keys from a hook on the wall. "What's on your checklist?"

"Something nondescript," I said.

Hannah gave us a wry smile. "In other words, no clown car."

It wouldn't surprise me to learn the woman had an actual clown car.

"I have a black sedan. Will that do?"

Callan offered a crisp nod. "Perfect."

She broke into a smile at the prospect of a deal. "You're in luck. It only has two hundred thousand miles on it."

"Great," I said.

She paused at the back door. "And only two missing hubcaps."

I tried to look on the bright side. "Who needs a hubcap?"

"And the front left is a spare tire," she added. "But very sturdy. Although the car does lean slightly to the left. But it's hardly noticeable."

"We'll make it work," I said.

Our saleswoman jingled the keys. "Excellent. I'll show you the car and we can fill out the paperwork."

Callan waved a hand. "I think we can dispense with the formalities." He pulled out a wad of bills and exchanged them for the keys. "Let's get this over with."

We followed her through the back door to a dirt-covered lot. Three cars were parked in a neat row. The first one was raised on stone blocks and missing all four tires. The middle car was missing the passenger door. The third car was our black sedan.

Hannah must've registered our horrified expressions because she said, "Eh, I've fallen on hard times. This is me making the best of a new opportunity."

"What did you do before this?" I asked. I could imagine Hannah doing any number of jobs—serving tables, operating a B&B, running a brothel...

"Worked as a fairy godmother for a spell," she said. "No pun intended."

Callan snorted. "There's no such thing."

Hannah looked at him askance. "Puns are a dime a dozen. What rock have you been living under?"

I touched his arm. "I think he means fairy godmothers."

"Oh, well. I'm not fae, of course. I'm a witch. Used to specialize in spells for the upwardly mobile. You know the type. Called myself a fairy godmother on my business cards as part of my branding."

"Very nice," I said.

"Clever, I thought. Anyway, times have been tough. The middle class has all but evaporated, so I was forced to seek other means of employment."

Callan's gaze swept the island of misfit cars. "And you chose *this*?"

"I sort of stumbled into the business. I was dating the previous owner, a fine man named Raymond. Then Raymond up and left me."

"Another woman?" I asked.

"No, he suffered a heart attack and dropped dead right in front of me." She shook her head. "Terrible tragedy. Then again, I should've realized I'd startle him greeting him the way I did."

"How did you greet him?" Callan asked.

Hannah lowered her lids. "Naked except for a cloak. I thought it would be a fun way to end the day. Instead I ended his life." She exhaled. "That was three years ago and I've been running this place ever since."

"I'm sorry to hear that," I said.

She waved me off. "It's all good. Life's a journey, not a destination. Sometimes you hit a few roadblocks."

"This is a minor setback," Callan said. "I wouldn't characterize it as a roadblock."

Her ruddy eyebrows crept up. "You said you're headed to Britannia City. If you take the main route, you're going to hit a major roadblock."

I exchanged an apprehensive glance with Callan. "Why? What's happening?"

"I'm surprised you haven't heard. Turf war between two wolf packs. Nasty situation. There won't be any left if they keep this up. One of them might win the battle, but they'll both lose the war."

Callan adjusted his sleeves. "We're more than capable of handling werewolves."

She shook her head. "I'm telling you—the highway is literally on fire. They're burning anything they can't control and the chaos is spreading fast."

"Does the king know?" I asked.

Although the question was directed to Callan, Hannah was the one who answered. "Beats me. If he does, I doubt he much cares. Wolves are expendable like the rest of us." Her gaze flicked to Callan. "Well, maybe not all of us."

"There must be another major route," I said. "One that gets us back to the city relatively quickly."

"Oh, sure. You can go through Birmingham. It's not as straightforward, but it'll be much faster for you under the circumstances."

Callan's shoulders tensed. "What about via Stoke-on-Trent?"

Hannah looked at him askance. "Why on earth would you go so far out of your way? Birmingham is bad enough. Have you ever heard the term 'Wild West'? It's like that, only with more tea."

"There has to be another way," he insisted.

When Callan was twelve, he single-handedly brought the city of Birmingham to its knees during his father's march to Britannia City. By all accounts, the city still hadn't recovered.

Hannah shrugged. "Usually I'd agree with you. Smart travelers avoid that area, but right now that means taking your chances with a dragon horde. They're blocking the other main artery. Apparently they're protecting a nest. We get them in Wales on occasion but a blocked road here has fewer repercussions." She slipped her thumbs through the empty belt loops of her pantsuit. "I don't envy House Lewis. They've got their work cut out for them."

"Indeed," Callan said. "Thank you for your help."

"Good luck, you two," she said and returned to the building.

I could tell by Callan's expression that he was actually debating the dragon horde option. "No," I said firmly. "We'll go through Birmingham."

"You know I can't do that." His jaw looked so rigid, I was surprised he could form words.

"I'll be right there with you." He wouldn't have to face his demons alone.

"Do you think that makes it better? I'm trying to keep you safe, not parade you through a danger zone."

"I'm a knight, remember? A sworn protector. I have magic you haven't seen." I winked at him, trying to keep the tone playful.

"And I'm the Beast of Birmingham, or have you forgotten?"

"I thought it was the Butcher."

His jaw remained clenched. "They call me a lot of things. None of them flattering."

"We'll drive straight through without stopping. They won't even know you passed through." I swiped the keys from his hand. "And I'm driving."

His eyes narrowed. "You can't drive, remember? That's why I had to drive the jeep in Devon."

"Technically it isn't that I *can't*. It's just that I don't have a lot of experience." Life in Britannia City didn't afford me many opportunities behind the wheel.

"Whereas I have plenty." He snapped his fingers for the return of the keys.

"You'll be distracted. Nobody needs an emotionally

charged driver behind the wheel. I'll focus on the road and you focus on not imploding."

He opened his mouth to argue but seemed to think better of it. "Fine. You win."

I cupped my ear. "A little louder for the people in the back."

Without a word, he yanked open the passenger door and slumped in the seat. His six-foot-four frame seemed to take up half the sedan.

I settled behind the wheel and adjusted the seat to fit my long legs. "Seatbelt," I ordered.

He glanced at his broad chest. "I think I'll be okay."

I leaned back. "I'm not starting this engine until everyone is strapped in and secure."

"Everyone?" He craned his neck to peer at the backseat. "Are we taking on passengers?"

"Seatbelt."

Grumbling, he fastened his belt. "Satisfied?"

"Rarely."

He smirked. "Sounds like a 'you' problem."

I started the engine, switched on the lights, and pulled onto the road. "I can't help it if my standards are high."

"I don't think it's that they're high. I think it's that they're warped."

"Warped is a strange word to use."

"Twisted? Misguided?"

I didn't particularly want to hear the vampire prince's assessment of my personal choices. "I need you to put your navigator hat on. I have no idea where I'm going."

He pointed at the windshield. "That way."

"Very helpful, Prince Magellan. Thank you."

Callan pressed a button on the dashboard and music filled the car. "Good, old-fashioned radio waves."

I didn't recognize the song. "Having it louder doesn't make it sound better, you know. Some of us need to concentrate on the road."

"You mean on learning to drive."

I shrugged. "You caved. You could've fought harder for dominance."

A predatory sound escaped him. "You'd like that, would you?"

My grip tightened on the wheel. "What's that? I can't hear you above the music."

He lowered the volume. "Spoilsport."

"Who's the band?"

Callan cracked the window and a cool burst of air invaded the cramped space. "You don't know Fleetwood Mac?" He seemed mildly incredulous.

"No, sorry. Should I?"

"If you have taste, then yes. They were a British-American rock band."

"The nineteen-seventies?" Their sound reminded me of other music I'd heard from that era.

"Close. They started in 1967 I believe." He looked at me. "Seems your mother missed out on historical music lessons."

"Guess so." I wasn't bothered by the alleged knowledge gap. She'd focused more on information that could save my life. Music wasn't going to keep me alive. Then again, neither was architecture and she'd taught me plenty about that. Personal preferences had leaked into her teachings, apparently. The revelation was somehow comforting. It meant I could learn more about my mother simply through what she chose to teach and what she chose to omit.

"Who taught you about music?" I asked.

He fell silent and I immediately regretted asking the

question. The moment stretched into several until I broke the silence.

"Your mother liked music?" I ventured.

He kept his gaze on the road ahead. "All kinds. Classical. Rock. Jazz."

"Did she play any instruments?"

"Piano. She tried to teach me, but my father shut that down quickly."

"What's wrong with the piano?"

"Nothing, but no son of his was going to be musical. I was being groomed for greater things."

"Couldn't you play both piano and Napoleon?"

He smiled. "And there's a history reference."

"Can't help it. It's in my blood." Literally.

He turned up the volume. "And music is in mine."

I went quiet and listened. One song changed to another and I felt like I'd gotten to know more about Callan in a single car ride than I had during our entire journey through Devon. Not just facts but something deeper. A glimpse into his soul.

Feeling ridiculous, I swore under my breath, which prompted a concerned look from Callan.

"Problem?"

"Sorry. That wasn't meant to be out loud." I sank against the worn leather seat. A glimpse into his soul? I had to alter my mindset quickly. He was still a vampire prince and I was still—me.

If I risked my heart, I'd risk my head too.

Callan fiddled with the buttons until he located another working radio station. "What do you think of this one?"

I listened to the beat. "This song I know. It's called Eau De Humanity." By the band Helen of Troy.

"So you're not completely clueless when it comes to music."

"The menagerie likes music, especially Big Red."

"You do have quite the collection, don't you?"

"Collection?" I shot him an outraged look. "They're not trinkets. They're living creatures."

"I didn't mean any offense. I think it's wonderful that you take care of them."

"It's either that or let them become a meal for someone."

"Right. You're a vegetarian."

"I am." And so was he, in a sense. My fingers tapped the wheel in time to the music as I waited to see whether he'd confess his efforts to fund a secret formula that replaced human blood.

"I suppose you disapprove of tribute centers, too, in that case," he said.

"It doesn't matter what I think, does it? I'm neither human nor vampire." Only half vampire and fortunately that half didn't require blood.

"You disapprove," he said matter-of-factly. "You disapprove of vampires in general. I remember how resistant you were to working with one when we first met. I had to beat you into submission."

I barked a laugh. "Are you insane? You did not beat me into submission. If anything, I beat you."

Now it was his turn to laugh. "Let's not argue. I find singing much more agreeable."

He hiked the volume and music seemed to permeate every fiber of my being. It was as though we'd discovered a new common language. We sang together—me out of key and Callan with what sounded to me like perfect pitch. Bastard. Did he have to be good at everything?

I lowered my window and sang even louder.

Callan burst into laughter. "Are you strangling cats over there?"

"Hey!" I sounded more aggrieved than I actually felt. I was, in fact, terrible. I didn't care though. I was enjoying myself too much.

We were having the kind of moment my mother used to call...I frowned, trying to recall the phrase. "Avoir la pêche," I said, relieved to have remembered.

Callan cut a glance at me. "Pardon?"

"It's something my mother used to say."

His mouth turned up a smidge at the corners. "To have the peach?"

"She used it to mean high spirits or a good day." I shrugged. "One of those moments that makes you feel great. She was fond of idioms in other languages."

"Your mother sounds exceedingly clever. And what made you think of it?"

"Must've been you talking about your mother's influence," I lied.

"Ah. I see." He was still smiling when he turned to face the windshield again.

I turned toward my driver's side window and allowed myself a small smile. Avoir la pêche indeed.

We arrived at the border crossing and waited our turn at the end of a long line of vehicles.

"Who knew so many people were eager to visit House Lewis territory?" I mused.

"They're probably headed to work. There's an employment pass that allows laborers to cross the border for their jobs. A lot of people who live in House Kane territory actually work in ours. The Houses have an employment treaty as well as a reciprocal tax treaty."

"I guess that's what happens when Houses get along. You don't have that with Peyton or Duncan, do you?"

He pulled a face. "Certainly not. Too much history."

"Not with Peyton though."

He gave me a dark look. "Not officially."

"Unofficially? I can understand your father, but why Peyton?"

"Because they were upset when my father chose his second bride from another House. They felt it should've been a member of their family. A cousin named Genevieve or some such name."

Queen Imogen was from House Osmond across the English Channel. Osmond was a stronger House than Peyton with a fleet of ships built to withstand encounters with sea monsters.

"And now they feel slighted again with you rejecting Princess Louise's advances." Louise had made her position perfectly clear, even sending two thugs to kill me during a royal event at the castle in Devon.

"It's Maeron they should be keen to secure for Louise. I'm still the heir to House Duncan."

"It is odd, isn't it?" Louise seemed sharp enough to know that Maeron was the smarter choice.

Callan's silence was deafening.

"Callan?" I prompted.

His head jerked toward me. "Sorry, I got distracted by the border agent. He's wearing the most ridiculous uniform. I'm embarrassed for him."

I squinted ahead to see a vampire wearing a crimson jacket with gold tassels hanging from the shoulders. "He looks like a bellhop."

"You should swap seats with me in case they give us a hard time."

"I'll stay put, thanks. They can see you just as clearly in the passenger seat."

He scowled. "You always need to dial up the difficulty, don't you?"

"Hey, it's not my fault there are turf wars and dragon hordes." I pulled up to the booth and rolled down my window. "Good day, sir."

The border agent held out a hand. "Passes, please."

Callan leaned across me. "Hello." He peered at the vampire's name badge. "Kevin, is it?"

Kevin's eyes rounded. "Yes, sir. I mean Your Highness." He attempted to bow and ended up whacking his forehead on the window ledge of the booth. "I'm a huge fan, Your Highness. The hugest."

"No need for formalities, Kevin," Callan said. "If you could wave us through, I'd appreciate it. We're rather pressed for time."

Kevin rubbed his wounded forehead. "I didn't receive word to expect you, Your Highness. Usually there's some sort of motorcade." His gaze lingered on the beat-up black sedan.

"He's traveling incognito," I said. "I'm a knight and I was in Wales on official business for House Lewis." I lowered my voice. "Highly confidential, hence the car."

Kevin nodded eagerly. "Completely understand. Good thing you decided to cross here. The other crossings are a mess what with the dragons and the werewolf situation."

"Yes, I'm pleased to see my intel was good." Callan smiled at him. "Thank you for being so diligent. I'll be sure to pass on a good word to the king."

Kevin puffed out his chest. "Many thanks, Your Highness." He raised the barrier and waved us through.

The engine stalled, but I managed to get us going again. Phew.

"Well done," I told him, once we were back on the road.

"Well done to you as well." He grinned at me. "We do make an excellent team."

"I never disputed that. I work as part of a team for a living. I'm very good at it."

"As do I, in my own way." He stopped talking, as though he said something he shouldn't have.

We rode for a while in companionable silence. It was nice to sit beside someone and not feel compelled to chat. The menagerie aside, Kami was the only one who didn't make me feel awkward about long silences. When you spend enough time in the tunnels with someone hiding from danger, you learn how to be comfortable in the quiet.

My stomach growled. "Let me know if you see anyplace good to stop for food."

"You can get something to eat once we're through the city. I don't think stopping is a good idea."

No, he wouldn't think that.

"Sounds like a plan," I said. "Keep an eye out for signs. I don't know which way to go next."

He pointed to the city looming in the distance. "There."

"This isn't a hover car. I can't drive straight across."

"Too bad." He paused to read the plethora of brightly lit signs along the road. "Keep right to reach the city center."

The car sputtered and died just outside of the city limits.

Because of course it did.

We took turns cursing and trying to identify the problem so we could fix it. It seemed to be the engine but all efforts to revive it failed. Even my magic proved useless. Finally Callan simply stood and stared at the engine.

"You can't intimidate an engine into working," I said.

"You'd be surprised." He dusted off his hands. "What now?"

I glanced at the cityscape. "Now we walk."

He grunted. "All the way to Britannia City? Someone's ambitious."

"Not all the way. We board a train in Birmingham."

He was quiet for a moment. "Yes, I think that makes sense."

"Wow. Someone quote the prince for posterity."

"We should've gone through Stoke-on-Trent."

I closed the car door not bothering to lock it. Let the thieves strip it for parts. It was no use to us now. "We're here now. No point in asking what if."

Drawing a deep breath, Callan stuffed his hands in his pockets and contemplated the city lights ahead. "This will be most unpleasant."

6

Callan and I walked along the streets of Birmingham with our heads down and our antennae up. Once upon a time, the city boasted three main railway centers, but Birmingham New Street was the only to survive and now simply called Birmingham Station. I'd heard the city described many times and not one of them was flattering. The Wild West but with tea, as Hannah said. Pedro had called it a werewolf wasteland and said most respectable vampires had abandoned it for more hospitable places. Looking at the litter that hugged the curbs and the neglected buildings, my current view was in line with those negative assessments.

"This was apparently the jewelry neighborhood before the Great Eruption," I said in an effort to keep Callan distracted from his demons. Returning to the city for the first time in twenty years had to be challenging for him.

He made a noncommittal sound in response.

We passed a window display featuring gold necklaces on headless mannequins.

"Looks like it still is," he said.

There weren't too many people out and about. The streets weren't as well-lit here as in Britannia City. I wondered whether the perpetual darkness contributed to the absence of shoppers, not that it mattered. The fewer city dwellers we passed, the less likely Callan would be recognized. We only had to make it to the train station without incident and then he could slump in a seat and stare out the window until we arrived at Britannia City. Invisibility was an option if necessary, but the vampire couldn't sustain that form long enough to reach the station. It was best to keep that option in reserve.

"You could shift into a butterfly if you want," I said. "That way you won't be noticed."

"I'm more vulnerable in my butterfly state." His tone left no room for argument.

Silence stretched between us. Walking beside him right now was like walking beside a cardboard cutout. The royal vampire seemed to have vacated his body but instructed the legs to keep moving.

"I'm sorry we have to go this way. I know this must be hard for you."

The cardboard cutout opened its mouth. "It's fine."

"It isn't fine and you don't have to pretend otherwise."

I surveyed the dilapidated buildings around us and tried to imagine what this place looked like twenty years ago before Callan unleashed his fury. Even if he hadn't personally leveled these particular shops, he'd been the catalyst for their demise.

Twelve years old. Birmingham must've scarred him as badly as it had scarred its inhabitants. The vampire prince seemed to only use a fraction of his power now. We were more alike than I realized.

"The less we talk, the faster we walk," he said gruffly.

I cut him a quick glance. More like the less we talked, the less he communicated his feelings.

"You could tell me about Dale. Might be a nice way to honor his memory." Callan had shared a story about a cousin who'd traveled with him en route to Britannia City but didn't survive. They'd been as close as brothers and it was Dale's death in Birmingham that had triggered Callan's infamous tirade.

He kept his gaze locked on the pavement. "You remember."

"Of course I remember. You lost someone you cared about very much." And I understood that acutely.

"Save your sympathy for someone who deserves it." He quickened his pace.

I hurried to catch up with his long strides, garnering a curious look from a passing werewolf. "Callan, you were only a boy." A boy who'd been manipulated by his abusive father into fighting in the name of power and greed. That wasn't the Callan I'd come to know. He was nothing like the Highland king.

"It's no excuse." He stopped abruptly to face me. "I let my emotions get the better of me that day. After seeing what I was capable of, I swore never again. In twenty years, I've only broken that rule once."

I folded my arms. "And where was that? I think I would've heard about another incident featuring the Demon of House Duncan."

The intensity of his gaze gave me goosebumps. "It wasn't a public spectacle."

"St. Paul's?" He'd killed several wizards when they attacked me there.

"No, I'm not talking about violence. I'm talking about emotions getting the better of me."

I gave him a blank look.

"Peyton Castle in Devon."

"Peyton Castle? But I was with you there."

Wordlessly he turned and continued walking.

A memory flashed in my mind of the guest bedroom in the castle's guest quarters. Callan's fingers tangled in my hair. His lips exploring my bare skin. His fangs scraping gently against the curve of my neck.

The night we nearly lost control.

I caught up to him again. "Are you really comparing a hot make-out session with the razing of a city?"

"I didn't raze the city. That's always been an exaggeration." He glanced at me. "Hot, huh?"

Any hotter and my body would have imploded, not that I'd share that with him. I was trying to ease his suffering, not fuel his royal ego.

"What happened in the castle...It was a bad idea," I said.

"We're in agreement on that."

I flinched. An argument would've been nice, however anemic.

We waited at a crosswalk for the light to change. I exhaled at the sight of the train station up ahead. Not far now.

"It can't be," a voice said, heavy with dismay. "Tell me this is a bad dream."

I turned to see a bald man shaking a cane at Callan. Tufts of white hair sprouted above his ears. His gums were visible, showing only a few teeth.

"You have quite a lot of nerve showing your face in these parts."

I placed a gentle hand on Callan's arm. "Let's keep walking."

"No." Callan's voice was barely a whisper. He pivoted to the old man. "Who did I take from you?"

The old man appeared taken aback by the blunt question. "You mean who'd you murder in cold blood?"

"Yes," Callan replied.

The old man blinked. "My son, Gary. You'd punched through a wall with such force, he was trying to keep it from collapsing on others. It fell anyway."

"I'm sorry," Callan said.

Brandishing his cane, the old man whacked the side of Callan's leg. "Oh, yes. I donated your apology. Wouldn't spend a single coin of your guilt money no matter how desperate I was. My son's life was worth more than you could ever give me."

Callan bowed his head. "If I could take it back, I would. Truly."

The old man lowered his cane. This interaction seemed to be going very differently from the way he'd imagined it.

"Gary was my only son," the old man said, sounding deflated. "He was just starting his life. Engaged to a lovely girl named Sally. She went on to marry someone else, but I know she can't be nearly as happy as she would've been with my Gary. My wife's five years gone now and I know it was from the heartache of it all. Took a horrible toll on her health." His voice thickened and he seemed to have trouble speaking.

Callan patted the old man's shoulder. "If it's any consolation, there isn't a single day that passes that I don't think of the victims and regret my choices."

The old man's brow furrowed. "I think you mean that."

Callan's face remained solemn. "I do."

The old man cast a furtive glance behind us. "I'm afraid now it's my turn to apologize."

"What could you possibly have to apologize for?" Callan asked.

The sound of pounding footsteps gave me a clue. Angry voices rolled toward us like thunder.

"You assembled a mob?" I demanded.

The old man patted his pocket where the shape of a phone bulged. "I sent a message as soon as I recognized you. There's a bounty on your head here, you know."

"This is House Lewis territory," I said. "How do you think the king will feel about his subjects attacking the prince?"

The old man spat on the pavement. "I'm afraid we don't think much of a king who would let a murderer live in luxury under his roof." He backed away. "If what you say is true, I am sorry. If it means anything to you at all, I forgive you."

Callan placed his palms flat against each other and bowed. "It means everything."

The old man hobbled away as the silhouette of a crowd surged toward us. We had to get out of here before they attacked or Callan would be earning his nickname all over again.

Callan snarled at the sight of them. "I don't want to fight."

"Maybe not, but they definitely want to fight you."

A wave of anger rushed toward us, palpable in its fury. Metal glinted and clothing shredded as fur exploded from the vengeful mob. The north remembered the Butcher of Birmingham and they were here to demand their two hundred and twenty pounds of flesh.

"There he is!" a deep voice rumbled.

A wolf howled in the distance. It sounded like a summoning.

I grabbed Callan's hand. "We can outrun them."

He stared at the approaching mob with a mixture of anguish and resignation. "I should let them air their grievances."

I spotted a crossbow in the crowd. "They're about to air their weapons."

"Can you blame them?"

I tightened my hold on his hand. "Letting them beat you to death won't change the past. Please, Callan. You can make reparations without offering yourself on a platter."

I turned invisible. He hesitated only briefly before following my lead and vanishing from sight.

A werewolf screeched to a halt at the corner, looking left to right. "Where'd they go?"

Together we bolted from the maddening crowd. There was no sense in trying to make amends with an angry mob. Callan would kill them all to defend himself.

Or he wouldn't—and that prospect was even worse.

The Callan I'd just glimpsed seemed to think he deserved whatever happened to him.

Not on my watch.

We arrived at the station and raced to the platform. The flashing sign said the train to Britannia City was leaving in five minutes. We didn't have five minutes. It didn't take a genius to figure out our destination. The crowd would find us.

We slipped onto the train and turned ourselves visible. Callan collapsed in a seat. I peered out the window to see the mob advancing toward the train. More werewolves had gone full furry. If they managed to get on this train, things would get ugly fast.

"Ward the doors and windows," I yelled.

A conductor glimpsed the approaching crowd and

sprang into action. I was relieved to see his hands glow with an orange light. A wizard was exactly what we needed. He used a spell to seal the doors and windows.

Callan stood. "It's wrong for me to hide."

I pushed him back into the seat. "You're not hiding. Now stop being a martyr. The world needs you."

I need you, I nearly said.

Nearly.

The carriage rocked back and forth as the angry mob pushed both sides.

"What do they want?" the conductor asked.

"Me," Callan said.

The conductor seemed to notice the vampire for the first time. His eyes widened. "You're *him*."

"By order of King Casek, this train is going to leave a couple minutes early," I said.

"Yes, ma'am." The conductor hurried to the front of the carriage and disappeared.

I turned my focus back to the crowd. The train wouldn't be able to leave if it wasn't properly on the tracks. With all their werewolf strength, this group could easily tip us. I had to do something.

I faced the crowd on the right side of the carriage and connected with my magic. I didn't want to hurt them, but I had to keep them away from the train long enough for us to depart.

Air magic should suffice. Once I gathered enough energy, I pushed outward. The metal between us was no barrier. The crowd dispersed like fallen pins at the end of a bowling lane. I ran to the left side of the carriage and performed the same magic again.

The whistle blew.

Thank the gods.

A few ambitious werewolves tried to hold on as the train began to move, but they couldn't gain purchase and slid to the platform. I watched until I was certain we were free and clear. Only then did I join Callan in a seat.

"I think you were right," I said.

"About what?"

"The dragon horde would've been preferable."

His smile was faint but it was there. Progress. "Thank you for your help."

"If it weren't for me, you wouldn't be here."

The conductor returned from the adjoining carriage. "All good, Your Highness?"

"Yes, thank you," Callan replied. "Why is this carriage empty?"

"It's the first-class carriage to Britannia City, Your Highness. No one can afford it."

Callan pulled three crisp bills from his pocket and handed them to the conductor. "For your trouble."

"It was no trouble at all, Your Highness. For once we didn't leave late." He tipped his cap and continued to the next carriage.

Callan stared out the window at the passing shades of gray. "I'm going to have a word with the king when I return to the palace."

"About the mob?"

"Birmingham in general. They're right to be upset. It's been twenty years and they've received very little to aid their recovery. No wonder so many have fled. We owe our subjects better than that."

"Do you think he'll agree with you?"

"I do." He turned to look at me. "I sense that you held back. That you could've done far more than a simple burst of air. What I don't understand is why."

"I didn't want to hurt them," I said.

His gaze lingered on me. "What I'd really like to know is how much damage you're truly capable of."

Given the circumstances, his remark surprised me. As events in Birmingham demonstrated, some things were better left a mystery.

I looked past him out the window. "Let's hope we never have to find out."

7

I sat on the sofa with Big Red curled on my lap and the other animals squished against my hips and ankles. They were thrilled to be back in the flat and had no trouble expressing their joy—all except Hera, of course. The cat saw fit to show her displeasure by promptly peeing in the bathtub. Sometimes it surprised me that cats didn't rise to dominance after the Great Eruption.

Now that I was home and safe, I couldn't stop thinking about what I'd learned at the Atheneum. Stunned didn't begin to cover it.

"So, big news. My father is a vampire king," I told the menagerie. Only Jemima seemed impressed. The hen pecked my arm slowly and gently instead of with her usual impatience. I assumed it was her way of showing reverence.

Sweet Davina was my half-sister. Prickly Maeron was my half-brother. Things could be worse. I could be related to Callan.

I forced my attention to the more urgent matter. As mind-blowing as my father's identity was, I wasn't about to announce it with a bullhorn at the palace door. The information wouldn't lead me to the two remaining stones either. Time to prioritize.

I rested my head against the sofa cushion and tried to conjure a memory of the visions from the Atheneum. From what I recalled, there didn't seem to be any easily identifiable landmarks, nothing that screamed *X marks the spot*.

"Maybe I should talk to the Green Wizard and see how much he knows," I said.

The Green Wizard's real name was Joseph Yardley, the leader of the People in Support of Ra. The organization was dedicated to eradicating vampires by bringing back the sun at any cost. It was the 'any cost' aspect I took issue with.

Multiple sets of eyes judged me. Harshly.

The goat bleated.

"Yardley wasn't the one who tried to sacrifice you," I told Herman. "That was a different misguided individual."

The Green Wizard had a team at his disposal. It was possible one of them was adept at research and could identify the place I'd glimpsed. Technically I had a team, too, but I felt uncomfortable dragging the banner into this mess. It would only endanger them and it wasn't as though we'd get paid for the trouble. Granted, keeping powerful stones out of the wrong hands was priceless, but I fully recognized this was a dangerous game I was playing. The other knights would volunteer their services simply because I asked and it wasn't fair to them. If I lost, I'd bring them down with me.

The sound of the buzzer jolted me to my feet. I hurried to the intercom and hit the button. "Yes?"

"Hey, it's Ione."

I buzzed her in and stayed by the door until she reached the top of the stairs.

"I wasn't sure if you were back," she said. "I've been trying to reach you, but the phones are down."

Typical. "What's going on?"

"I need an assist. Everybody else is out except Minka and you know how she is."

I knew. Minka Tarlock would much rather wield a pen than a sword. For a witch with decent magical skills, she was surprisingly risk averse.

I reached for my axe that I'd left propped against the wall. "Where are we headed?"

Ione pressed her lips together. "A job."

"That's very insightful. And where is this job?"

"You're not going to like it."

"That's obvious from your expression. Where?"

She exhaled. "Martin Lane."

"Terrific."

Martin Lane was one of the oldest streets in the city and also one of the most dangerous. Well, if I wanted to keep my mind off my warped feelings for Callan and my heritage, this was a golden opportunity.

"Seven Bells?" I asked.

"Yep."

I strapped on my axe and we left the flat together.

Martin Lane was close to the Thames, southwest of the old Monument tube station. The Seven Bells building dated back to 1663. Originally a merchant's house, it later became a pub but changed names and ownership several times over since then. The building survived the Great Fire in 1666, world wars, and, of course, the Great Eruption. Some said it was blessed. Others claimed it was cursed—that the owner had struck a deal with a demon and that was the only reason it remained standing. The main thing to know about Seven Bells was that it had a tunnel that connected the cellar to the river. Once used by smugglers, the route was now used by monsters to sneak up from the Thames to terrorize an unsuspecting public. You would think Seven Bells would be empty as a result, but you would be wrong. Patrons flocked to the pub in the hope of being present when a creature reared its head—or multiple heads, depending on the monster.

Ione and I entered the pub and approached the counter where a portly, balding man was pulling pints.

"Are you Glenn?" Ione asked.

Nodding, the man wiped his hands on a plain white apron. "Mr. Hancock hired you?"

"Yes, we're from the Knights of Boudica," she replied.

The man puffed out his cheeks. "Thank goodness. I've been waiting for you. The boss doesn't want me to shut down early, but I was sorely tempted."

A quick survey of the pub showed no obvious problems. There were plenty of patrons and servers running to and fro.

"What's so bad that you'd want to close early?" I asked.

His gaze drifted to the floor. "Down there," he whispered.

Well, that wasn't ominous. Not at all.

"Any idea what it is?" I asked. "The more information we have before heading down, the better."

"None. I caught a glimpse of movement down there earlier when I went to bring up another barrel. Much too big for a rat."

"Nothing attacked you?" Ione asked.

Glenn shook his head. "Kept to the shadows, which is one of the reasons I got nervous. The dumb ones don't stay hidden."

He wasn't wrong.

"You think it came from the river?" Ione asked.

"Seems likely. I noticed wet patches on the floor this

morning, but I didn't think anything of it at the time. Sometimes things leak and the cellar is always damp."

"Any strange noises?" I asked.

"No. Whatever it is, it's quiet and hasn't attacked the inventory. We had a baby hydra down there once and it made a complete mess of the boxes and barrels. You could hear the ruckus from across the street." He angled his head to the right. "You might also want a word with that young lady at the corner table. She wandered downstairs by accident to find the loo."

Ione's eyes rounded. "She saw something?"

"Says it's a ghost, but I suspect she saw the same thing I did."

I followed his gaze to the young woman seated at a small table with two young men. She looked about sixteen with electric blue hair tied in pigtails and piercings in her nose, ears, and tongue. "She's still here, so I guess whatever it was didn't freak her out too badly."

"Most of our clientele are here for a potential sighting. Problem is most of them don't realize they'll piss their pants when it actually happens."

Ione's laughter mingled with mine.

"If they're that interested, they can become knights," I offered.

"Or travel to South America," Ione added. South America had been hardest hit by the Great Eruption and the world had collectively decided to abandon the continent to the monsters.

"Most folks that come in here aren't cut out for a banner," Glenn said. "They're just looking for a temporary thrill. Same as going to an amusement park or trying to ride a wild dragon."

Most people who tried to ride a wild dragon ended up dead. Not quite the thrill they intended.

"Where's the cellar entrance?" Ione asked.

Glenn pointed to the doorway closest to the blue-haired girl's table.

"We'll let you know what we find," I said.

Glenn's gaze darted across the room. "Whatever you do, try to keep it down, would you? No need to create a panic situation. The boss will take any lost business out of my wages."

"We'll do our best," Ione said.

"No promises," I muttered. Monsters were like toddlers. Hard to predict and even harder to control.

We stopped when we reached the table nestled in the corner.

"Glenn tells us you saw something in the cellar," I said to the young woman. Her eyes were an unnatural amber color. Had to be colored contact lenses.

"Quite certain it was a ghost," she replied. "That's what we're here to see anyway, so it worked out. I tried to get these two clowns to go back down there with me, but the manager said no."

"You told the manager first?" I asked.

"He saw me come up from the cellar and asked me what I was doing. They really need better signage if they want me to find the restroom more easily."

"Can you describe what you saw?" I asked.

"It was only a shadow."

The blonde beside her jostled her with his elbow. "You said it was eight feet tall."

"A tall shadow," she corrected herself.

"Slender or muscular?" I asked.

She scrunched her nose. "It was a shadow. How was I supposed to tell?"

"Was the shadow wide and lumpy or tall and straight?" I pressed.

She pursed her lips, appearing to mull it over. "Lumpy."

"How many heads?" I asked.

The young men laughed, but their smiles quickly faded when I repeated the question.

"You're serious?" the blonde asked.

Ione cocked her head and examined him. "Do we live in the same city?"

"These two live in bubble wrap," the girl said. "That's why we're here. I wanted them to have an experience."

I wouldn't wish this kind of 'experience' on anyone. These kids had no idea how dangerous Martin Lane could be.

"You don't think it's a ghost down there?" the second guy asked.

Ione glanced at the darkened doorway. "Could be. I've heard there are still skeletons buried in the cellar."

"Doubtful," I said. "I'm sure they've been picked over by the monsters by now."

"But the ghosts would still be here," the girl interjected. "Monsters can't eat ghosts."

I shrugged. "Depends on the monster."

The girl frowned. "Which monsters eat ghosts?"

Ione clasped my hand and tugged. "Let's go before you frighten away the patrons and upset our client."

We stepped through the doorway and descended the staircase to the cellar.

Glenn was right about the dampness in the air. The temperature dropped at least five degrees between upstairs and the cellar. The low ceiling was lined with wooden beams which surprisingly hadn't rotted from the constant moisture. They were likely spelled.

I peered around the stacks of crates in the direction of the tunnel. "Why don't we explore the cellar first and then head through the tunnel?"

Ione strung her bow. "Sounds good to me."

Metal clattered on the floor behind us and I twisted to glare at the blue-haired girl and her friends. "You shouldn't be here. Go upstairs."

"We want to see a monster," the blonde said.

How stupid were they? "Where do you live?" I asked. And could I afford to rent a place there?

"Hackney," the girl said.

Right. That explained it.

"Let me guess. Your families are AB-negative," Ione said.

The blonde nodded. "I'm not, just my parents and my sister."

So he reaped the rewards without sharing the burden. Lucky him.

The girl rolled up her sleeve to show off a pattern of small marks along her bare arm. "My blood goes straight to the palace. It's that special."

Inwardly I cringed.

"Don't make a face," the girl said.

Okay, maybe not so inwardly.

"We live a very good life," the girl continued. "Totally worth the temporary discomfort."

"Tell that to the people who don't survive," I shot back.

Across the room, a crate crashed to the floor.

"Holy hellfire," the blonde said, pointing.

"Upstairs," I yelled. "Now." I couldn't babysit three idiots while catching a monster.

Ione loosed an arrow. It sailed straight through the crack

in a crate. A creature wailed. It sounded like a dying seal—if that dying seal were ten times its normal size and had a trumpet where its mouth should be.

The teen trio screamed.

Ione whipped around to glare at them. "Up-effing-stairs. Now."

"You'd better go," I advised. "When Ione fake curses, shit's about to get real." The teens were holding on to each other for dear life. "I know you're here to see a ghost today, but if you don't leave now you're going to become one."

That did the trick. They ran up the stairs, practically knocking each other over in their effort to escape.

Ione and I hurried to confront the monster behind the crates but found only a small pool of blood.

"Where is it now?" Ione whispered.

I spotted droplets of blood at the tunnel entrance. "I think it went back toward the river." Not ideal. If the monster managed to get back in the water, we might lose it only to have it return another day.

"You first?" Ione asked.

I nodded and raced to the tunnel.

The monster hadn't returned to the river. Instead the bastard was waiting for me.

The creature swung its head toward me like a baseball bat and knocked me backward. The back of my head cracked against the hard floor.

At least I caught a glimpse of it before it attacked. Its head and body shape were whale-like but it used its fins like feet. It was a cetus, named after the sea monster that Poseidon sent to devour Andromeda. Cetus were surprisingly nimble and agile given their awkward shape and size. They were also highly intelligent.

"It's a cetus," Ione's voice rang out. She shot another arrow at the monster and nicked its blubbery coat.

"Thanks for the update." I scrambled to my feet and wrenched the axe from its sheath. Before I could swing, the cetus used its head to knock the weapon from my hand. The axe slid across the floor and landed in a puddle.

"If Babe gets rusty, you're going to regret it."

The cetus positioned itself between me and the axe.

Ione's next arrow missed its mark. The cetus opened its enormous mouth and sprayed us both with dirty water it had likely swallowed in the Thames. Tiny fish flapped on the floor and Ione spit one from her mouth. At least they were only small fish. Cetus were known to eat small animals and children too.

I surprised the creature by rushing toward it. At the last second, I dropped to the wet floor and slid to my axe. I scooped up Babe and returned to an upright position while still sliding. I skidded to a halt and whirled around to face the monster. It wailed in protest.

I raised the axe and threw it overhand. The blade buried itself in the monster's blubbery exterior. The cetus thrashed, knocking against Ione in the process. She bounced off the creature's body with such force, she flew across the room and crashed into a stack of crates. One by one they fell on top of her.

The cetus tried in vain to remove the axe. I focused inward and connected to my magic, feeling the imaginary key as it turned and unlocked my potential.

I'd encountered a cetus only once before. It had terrorized a fishing community near the English Channel. By the time the creature was killed, it had managed to eat two months' worth of the community's already-limited resources.

A humming sensation filled my body, causing my skin to tingle. My mind flashed to the explosion of silver light that had defeated the berserkers on Romeo's rooftop. I couldn't release that kind of power here. There was no telling what kind of damage that would do in a confined space like this. I could end up caving in the tunnel and destroying a pub that had managed to survive centuries. No thanks.

I whipped the air into a frenzy and concentrated on creating a funnel to contain the cetus. I'd done this move with water magic, but I found air more challenging to work with, especially in a confined space. Too much wind could destroy the pub's inventory.

I wrapped the air around the cetus and focused on moving it in a counterclockwise direction. The cetus lifted off the floor, immobilized by the funnel. An arrow shot straight through the funnel and struck the cetus in the chest. Another arrow quickly followed, penetrating the monster's eye. The creature's head lolled to the side.

I craned my neck to look at Ione. She stood on a stack of crates with another arrow ready to fire.

"I think you got it," I said. I released my hold on the funnel and it dissipated. The cetus fell to the floor in a heap.

Ione hopped down from the crates. "Better vantage point up there." She walked over to examine the monster. "What now?"

I glanced to the tunnel. "Drag it out to the river, I guess. Might as well leave it as food for other creatures." Circle of life and all that.

I grabbed its head and my hands quickly slipped off the slick surface. The monster's head slammed on the floor.

"It really needs shoulders," Ione said.

"File that in your report. Further evolution required." I pulled the fins at the monster's base. "A little help, please."

Ione joined me and together we dragged the monster through the tunnel and disposed of it in the river. Hauling herself backward, she sank against a wall.

"How are you not exhausted?" she asked. "My legs are ready to fall off and you look ready to run a marathon."

"I'm tired too," I lied. "I just hide it better." Using magic didn't exhaust me. Fighting not to use it was the real problem.

We returned to the main room of the pub, which was now empty.

"Glenn?" I called.

His balding head popped up from behind the bar. His face was drained of color and beads of sweat dotted his brow. Poor guy.

"Heard the ruckus, did you?" I asked.

He nodded profusely. "What was it?"

"A cetus," I told him. "Ever have one of those before?"

He shook his head. "Never even heard of it. How dangerous?"

"If it got hungry enough, it would've killed everyone in the pub and then continued to the rest of the buildings on the street," I said.

He swallowed hard. "Are there more?"

"Lucky for you they tend to travel solo," I said.

He lifted his apron to wipe the sweat from his face. "I'll tell the boss."

"Tell him to ward the tunnel while you're at it," Ione said.

"He won't. Bad for business. We do double the business of the Pig and Poodle down the street. The occasional monster adds to the pub's popularity."

I gave him a sharp look. "It's going to add to the pub's body count if he isn't careful. Another incident like this and you'll be scaring customers away instead of drawing them in."

Glenn nodded. "I've tried to tell him. I've threatened to quit more times than I can count."

"Why haven't you?" Ione asked.

"Need the work, of course." He rubbed his cheeks. "Maybe you could talk to him. Encourage him to hire a witch. I know one who acts as a consultant. She'd write up a proposal based on a tour of the pub and tell us how much it would cost to put protections in place."

"I can do that for you," I said.

Glenn's brow lifted. "No extra charge?"

"I'm already here. As far as I'm concerned, it's a public service."

"Much obliged," Glenn said. He looked ready to burst into tears.

"If your boss wants to hire us to implement any of the suggestions, tell him to call Minka and make an appointment."

"Thanks, I will." Glenn pulled a pint for himself and drank. "How about you? I think you could each use a pint after that."

Ione laughed. "I could use a pitcher after that, but we don't drink on the job."

"I used to say the same, but life's too short." Glenn chuckled nervously as he brought the glass to his lips. "Cheers."

8

Despite my reservations, I decided to meet with Joseph Yardley to see what he might know about Friseal's Temple and compare it with my own information from the Atheneum. The Green Wizard had gotten wind of the Elemental Stone before me, which was how our paths first crossed at the excavation site that was once St. Paul's Cathedral. Maybe he knew more than he'd let on. I'd have to choose my words carefully because I didn't want to compete with his organization for the remaining two stones. They were Yardley's men that Callan had killed at St. Paul's. The skilled wizards had been determined to get their hands on the Elemental Stone, attacking me in the process. Yardley's teleportation skills had allowed him to escape the encounter unscathed.

We arranged to meet at a tea shop near Covent Garden. Yardley didn't strike me as someone who'd be comfortable in Hole and I wanted to grease the wheels. If that took a full-leaf pyramid bag that smelled like cinnamon and classical background music, then so be it.

I positioned myself in a chair facing the door with my

back to the wall and awaited his arrival. He promised to come alone and tell no one. I didn't need any of his acolytes eavesdropping on our conversation and spreading the word.

A gray-haired woman bustled over to the table. She wore a yellow apron over a floral dress. Wrinkles lined her face. My mother told me that there was a time when women tried to smooth their wrinkles through surgery or by injecting chemicals into their skin. In the current world, wrinkles were a sign of perseverance. If you lived long enough to acquire them, you were doing pretty well.

"Can I get you anything, love?"

When she rolled up her sleeves, I noticed the marks. They trailed up both arms. If you didn't know any better, you'd think they formed a pattern you didn't understand.

But I understood.

She caught my expression and immediately tugged her sleeves back to their original position.

"I'm sorry," I said. I didn't want to embarrass her, but at the same time, it seemed insensitive to let the moment pass unacknowledged.

"No matter. I've survived every donation, which is more than I can say for my sister." She managed a weak smile. "Besides, they won't take me again. When you get to be my age, they think your blood tastes stale." Her smile faded. "Now what can I get for you?"

"I'll wait for my friend if you don't mind," I said.

She offered a curt nod and stopped at a nearby table before returning to the counter.

The door swung open and the Green Wizard crossed the threshold. He was an unassuming man with his hood up, likely part of the reason he managed to fly under the royal radar. It was only when he lowered the hood and you spotted the giant tattoo of a yellow sun on his shaved head that you knew you were dealing with a zealot.

Yardley's gaze landed on me and he approached the table, unsmiling. He unfastened his trademark green cloak and draped it over the back of the wooden chair.

"Thank you for coming."

He slotted his fingers together on the table and peered at me. "To say I'm intrigued would be an understatement."

The woman returned to the table when she spotted my companion. "A pot to share?"

"Excellent. Any scones, Miss...?" Yardley asked.

"The name's Helen. No cream this week, sadly. There's a supply issue, but we do have scones if you're tempted."

"Jam will do." He looked at me for approval.

"Sounds good to me. Thank you, Helen."

She smiled at Yardley with dimpled cheeks and bustled away to make the tea.

Yardley glanced around the room. "Very civilized, Miss Hayes. I like your style."

"Caught a show the other day and was worried you were the star. Turned out to be some other guy with a sun tattoo."

He nodded solemnly. "I knew Thornhill."

"One of yours?"

"Up until last year. He was too rash and we revoked his membership card."

"There are cards? I feel slighted."

His mouth turned up at the corners. "I highly doubt you invited me here to discuss my organization. You know where our meetings are held."

"You're right. I'm not much of a joiner. I'd like to talk to you about the Elemental Stone."

His smile stretched. "I'm all ears."

"There was a small group at your last meeting discussing

the stone. Someone insisted you had to have elemental magic already in your DNA in order to harness the stone's power. How would they know that?"

Helen delivered a pot of tea and two cups, along with two scones and a small ramekin of blackberry jam.

"Thank you," Yardley and I said in unison.

Helen seemed to sense we were having an important conversation and didn't linger.

Yardley smeared jam across every available inch of his scone.

I reached across the table and tapped a bare spot. "Don't miss there. That's valuable real estate."

He smiled and spread jam across the remaining visible part of the scone. "Jam is a luxury I'm not often afforded." He bit into the scone. "They knew because we kept track of the effects of the stone as well as who was in control of it at the time. We hypothesized from there."

I poured tea from the pot. "What else do you know about the stone?"

He chewed thoughtfully. "You did say 'stone,' right? Because I probably know more about a scone."

I sipped my black tea. "Stone."

"I believe stones like that one are the building blocks of the supernatural world and there are more to be found."

I nearly choked on my tea. "What makes you say that?"

"I believe we acquired our powers from the earth's core, where the stones were created."

Slightly off the mark. I was both disappointed and relieved.

Yardley continued chewing. "I believe only those who possess the potential for the abilities can benefit. The stone acts as a key that unlocks latent power. You need the right genetic material to start with or it won't work. There has to be a connection to begin with."

Based on what I knew, that part seemed accurate. The Immortality Stone benefitted vampires. The Elemental Stone enhanced the powers of those with elemental magic in their genetic makeup. The Transcendence Stone affected supernaturals with shifting abilities.

"But you no longer think possession of the Elemental Stone will enable you to bring back the sun?" That was the reason they'd hunted it initially.

He looked me straight in the eye. "Not a single stone, no. We need to find more."

"Where are you looking for them?"

He dusted the crumbs from his chin. "I have a team on the task. As soon as we learn where other elemental stones might be buried, we'll recover them."

Other elemental stones. I didn't have the heart to tell him there was only one left and it was in my possession.

"If we can harness the power of all the stones combined, we might be able to bring back our beloved sun and send vampires back to the shadows where they belong."

"I hate to break the news, but I don't think the stones would be capable of that kind of magic. They might be an incredible weapon in your bid to overthrow the vampires, but I don't see how they can rid us of the Eternal Night."

Yardley clenched his hand into a fist. "When we acquire them, we'll find a way."

Definitely a zealot, believing his own hype. Even if the group managed to claim all five stones and found they couldn't return the sun, then what? Yes, the stones would provide them with an incredible weapon against the vampires, but the vampires would still be powerful foes.

The group could end up causing an all-out supernatural war where there were no winners.

"You know what happens in every single story where people tried to build a tower to the heavens," I told him. "Didn't quite make it as high as the sun before they got smited big time."

Yardley nodded. "They were ambitious. I admire that."

"They must've been charming too. No one builds a coalition without a degree of personality."

He drank his tea and set down the cup. "Might've been intimidation or slavery."

I nibbled the scone. "You have a way with people."

A smile tugged at his lips. "Are you suggesting I build a coalition?"

"I think you're already doing it."

"And what about you, Miss Hayes? You don't feel equipped to band supernaturals together to overthrow vampire rule?"

"You should probably whisper when you ask treasonous questions." For all we knew, Helen was a vampire informant and that was the real reason she no longer had to give donations.

He snorted. "You don't manage to avoid detection for as long as I have without being able to assess a situation. I assure you our discussion here is safe."

I polished off the last of the scone and leaned back against the chair. "Here's the deal. I don't want to compete with you."

"Then join forces with me. We shall find the stones together."

"I'm not sure that's the right answer." He wasn't even barking up the right temple.

Yardley regarded me with interest. "Is this because of

your personal relationship with certain members of House Lewis?"

I blanched. "It's because I'm not sure immense power belongs in one pair of hands."

He reached across the table and clasped my hands in his. "Then let us make it two pairs."

I eased my hands away and set them on my lap. "I want to see the sun as much as anyone, but I'm not sure your plan is the answer."

He peered at me. "If I'm right and these stones are the building blocks—how can they not be powerful enough to rid the world of vampires? To allow us to start over and build the world anew."

"There's still so much we don't know."

"Think about it, Miss Hayes. No more tribute centers."

No more humans as walking juice boxes. No more illegal magic.

No more death sentences for dhampirs.

"I have thought about it, more than you know."

"As I've told you before, if you're not with us, you're against us. If we do not share the same objective…"

"We do. It's the method I'm unsure about." I tipped back my cup and finished the last of my tea. "If we're fighting each other, then we're weakening ourselves against our common enemy."

It was hard to think of House Lewis as my enemy though. Vampires as a species, maybe. But House Lewis? Good grief, they were technically my family.

The world was already a complicated place and my trip to the Atheneum had made it worse.

Yardley shrugged. "It would be an unfortunate outcome for both of us."

I pushed away my empty cup and plate. "I think we're going to have to agree to disagree."

My phone buzzed on the table. At least they were working again. I glanced at the screen to see Minka's name. "Excuse me for one second." I clicked the screen and brought the phone to my ear. "Hayes."

"Apparently you're late to meet a client. He's waiting for you at Hole and he sounds deeply unhappy...and also very attractive."

"He *sounds* attractive?"

"Never mind. Just get over there. I don't want you to sully our banner's reputation by being tardy."

"Minka, I don't have anything on the schedule..."

She didn't wait for me to finish before disconnecting the call. I stared at the phone in disbelief.

"Duty calls," I said to Yardley.

"I imagine it often does when you're a knight."

"How about a truce for now?"

He extended his hand across the table. "Let's put a pin in it, as they say."

We shook hands and I reached for my pocket. Yardley waved me off.

"My treat. It's a business expense, you see. Vampires have their downsides, but tax deductions aren't one of them."

Good to know.

I rose to my feet and started toward the door.

"Miss Hayes?"

I twisted to look at him.

"Do be careful out there. We can't possibly be the only ones in search of these stones."

No, we certainly weren't. "You, too," I said and left.

9

I showed up at Hole expecting to meet an annoyed client. Instead a familiar vampire sat in my booth.

Maeron.

That explained why the message came from Minka and not Mack. I usually met his spillover clients here, not ones from my regular banner.

"This is unexpected," I said, sliding into the seat opposite the vampire prince. I was surprised he bothered to arrange a fake meeting at all when he could've just as easily sent his minions to collect me.

"I hope you don't mind."

"Why would I possibly mind?" I signaled to George, who looked mildly disturbed by the sight of a royal vampire in his pub. Unlike Callan, Maeron hadn't bothered to disguise himself. He even wore a shirt with the royal insignia.

I squelched the urge to scrutinize him for any sign of our shared DNA. I offered an easygoing smile instead. "If vampires keep showing up here to meet me, I'm going to get a reputation."

"As someone with connections, I presume."

"Sure. Let's go with that."

George approached the table with caution, wiping his hands on the white towel draped over his shoulder.

"We'll share a pitcher of Barrel of Monkeys, George," I said.

Maeron arched a smooth eyebrow. "Will we now?"

"I sampled your royal wine. Now you can taste what the other half drinks."

George nodded and shuffled back to the counter to fill the order. I briefly considered ordering a vodka tonic so George could substitute a glass of water instead, but Maeron wouldn't be so easily fooled.

I folded my hands and gave him my full attention. "So, what brings you to my stomping grounds? You must realize how out of place you are."

"Out of place in my own territory?" With precise movements, he unfolded a white cloth napkin and set it on his lap. "I'd like to know more about your trip. Sounds like it was quite a fruitful one."

"I don't know what trip you mean."

He wagged a finger at me. "Come now, Miss Hayes. We both know you were in House Kane territory."

I frowned, momentarily taken off guard. "Callan told you?"

Smiling, he met my gaze. "Does that surprise you? My brother and I share many confidences, Miss Hayes." His fangs seemed to grow longer with each syllable. "And I do mean many."

There was no way Callan would betray my confidence. This had to be a trick.

"Why not invite me to the palace or the townhouse to discuss this?"

"I thought you'd be more comfortable in a place like

this." He gestured to the bar. "As you put it, your stomping grounds."

I maintained a friendly expression. "Well, the weather was damp and chilly and the food left a lot to be desired. What else would you like to know about Wales?"

His smile evaporated. "You've had such luck finding what's been lost. I was hoping for a repeat performance."

Then it hit me. Callan hadn't told him anything. Maeron knew because he was the one who'd sent two vampires to the Atheneum. Two vampires who'd returned empty-handed—and one empty-armed—but with a detailed description of me.

George returned with a pitcher and two pint glasses and set them on the table.

"Thank you, George." I fixed the vampire with a blank expression. "Who's lost? Princess Davina isn't missing again, is she?"

"I'm talking about objects." His lip curled as I poured from the pitcher. I made sure to slide the full glass over to him and pour a second one for me.

"What exactly would you like to know, Your Highness? I'm not very good at guessing games." I gulped the golden liquid and watched with amusement as he brought the glass to his mouth and cringed.

"What did you find in Wales?" He took a reluctant drink and grimaced. Oh, to be a spoiled vampire prince and never know the taste of cheap ale.

"I imagine the information is similar to what's in Antonia's book." *And here we go.*

He perked up. "Who's Antonia?"

"Antonia Birch. The museum curator who was murdered by one of Romeo's minions. He stole her book which then mysteriously vanished by the time we searched

Romeo's penthouse for it." I folded my arms. "I don't suppose you know anything about that."

Maeron ducked his head and chuckled. "You never cease to surprise me, Miss Hayes. I can see why my brother is so besotted."

"What's surprising? That I figured out your involvement or that your brother is besotted with a commoner like me?"

He spread his arms wide. "Can it be both?"

I swiped my glass from the table and took another long drink. Although I didn't necessarily want the alcohol, I did want to maintain my composure. Drinking seemed the easiest way to accomplish this goal because my insides were quivering. I may have faced off against a lot of monsters in my life, but not one of them was as lethal and calculating as Prince Maeron of House Lewis. He was his mother's son through and through.

"Why did you put me on the restricted travel list? Wouldn't it have been easier to let me go and have me followed like you did in Devon?"

"I wanted to be certain my men got to the information first."

"Top marks for effort." In for a penny, in for a pound. "Why did you have Romeo killed?"

The prince burst into laughter. "I believe that's called leaping to conclusions."

I leveled him with a look. "There's no leaping involved. I know you did."

He leaned forward. His breath smelled like a strange mixture of ale and peppermint. "Then surely you must know why."

"To keep him quiet. Once you extracted the information you wanted from him, you had to silence him."

Maeron kept his voice low and injected a hint of steel

into it. "I couldn't possibly allow a member of the pack to be privy to such valuable information. Wolves are enough of a blight on society without giving them more power."

"You told Callan that you searched Romeo as well as his penthouse and there was no stone."

His face hardened. "So did you."

"Maybe we're both telling the truth."

"The library frowns upon damage to their property, you know." I had no doubt he'd sent someone to find information on the temple and destroy all evidence of its existence.

"As a prince of House Lewis, their property is technically my property," he reminded me.

"It's a shame those books didn't have the information you were looking for. Would've saved your men a trip."

Maeron's frustration seemed to grow with each exchange. "I'll ask again. What did you learn in Wales?"

"Always travel with an extra layer. The temperature was much colder than I anticipated. Then again, I was on a mountain. I should've known."

Maeron snarled. "Let's leave the cute banter to you and my brother, shall we?"

"Davina says she finds it entertaining."

"That's because Davina is a teenaged girl," he ground out.

"You say that like it's an insult." I clucked my tongue. "Your sister would be very unhappy to hear you right now." *Our* sister.

"Is this how you handle all your assignments, Miss Hayes? Talk your opponents to death?"

I switched gears. "Why are you having Callan followed?"

Maeron's eyebrows drew together. "I don't have a death wish, Miss Hayes, which I most certainly would if I opted to have my brother followed."

If he was faking surprise, he was a better actor than I realized.

"Callan said someone's been following him." I refused to offer more. Now that I knew what Maeron had done, I assumed Callan felt I was in danger from Maeron.

He rubbed the pads of his fingers along the side of the glass. "I can assure you that I've done no such thing. My brother and I have our differences, but we don't spy on one another."

"Why don't you ask him about Wales?"

"Because he wasn't the one who entered the Atheneum." The screen of his phone brightened, drawing his attention. He frowned and shifted his attention back to me. "Enough games. I'd like the stone now."

Stone, singular. At least he hadn't figured out I possessed more than one.

I maintained a neutral expression. "What stone? There was no stone in Wales."

"Please don't embarrass yourself. Just before his untimely demise, Mr. Rice told me you took the stone from him."

"The only reason Romeo told you that was to screw with me. I'm sure he was very unhappy to learn I survived his attack dogs and thwarted his plan."

"Plausible but untrue."

"People lie under duress, Your Highness. They'll say anything to make the pain stop." And I had no doubt Romeo had endured his share of torture before he left this earthly plane.

Maeron ran a finger around the rim of his glass. "We administered a truth serum, Miss Hayes. There was no torture involved. He said one of your feathered friends took the stone from him."

"And I never saw the bird again. Usually they follow instructions but that one flew off with the bag Romeo was holding." I shrugged. "I don't know what was in it. I shouldn't have used a random bird. Lesson learned."

"I see."

Right now those were the two most ominous words I'd ever heard him utter. I shifted uncomfortably.

A moment passed and he flashed one of his charming smiles. "Why not work together the way you and my brother did in Devon?"

There was something in his intonation that rubbed me the wrong way.

"Those were special circumstances," I said. It was the closest I was willing to get to saying 'not in this lifetime or any other.'

"Ah, I'm not special enough, am I? I must confess, it's the first time a woman's told me that."

"It isn't that I don't want to help you. I just don't have what you need."

His gaze lingered on the exposed curve of my neck. "Oh, I'm not so sure about that."

What would he think of Callan and Adwin's plan? I couldn't imagine he'd jump on the synthetic bloodwagon.

"I quite like the idea of working together," he continued.

"Too bad I have nothing to offer."

"On the contrary. You have information as well as the stone. In fact, the reason I asked you here is to allow my team time to search your flat."

Every muscle in my stomach tightened. "My flat is warded."

His mouth twitched. "Impatience breeds creativity."

My fingers curled into fists. "What did they do?"

"Where is the stone?" he demanded.

My heart pounded and my palms broke into a sweat. "There are innocent animals in that flat. Innocent people who live in that building."

"And there still are. Whether that remains so, however, depends entirely upon you."

It was good to know my half-brother took after his mother rather than our father. It would make it easier on me when I killed him later.

"The stone isn't there."

His dark eyes alone threatened to do horrible things to me. "Then where is it?"

"I don't know."

He slammed a hand on top of the table. As much as I wanted to flinch, I held it together. If I showed weakness, he'd steamroll straight over me without a backward glance.

I played the best card I had. "How do you think your brother would feel about you threatening me?"

"Do you really think he'll believe the word of a parasitic knight over mine?"

"You said yourself he's besotted with me. Men do strange things when they're besotted."

His fangs glinted in the dull light. "I was merely being polite. Do you honestly think he's been avoiding you to keep you safe? It's only an excuse, my dear. A way of disentangling himself without appearing to be the bad guy. When you spend years trying to repair a tarnished reputation..." He shook his head mournfully. "He doesn't want to be seen as mistreating a woman, particularly a knight. His behavior is merely to save face."

So Maeron knew that Callan was avoiding me to keep me safe. What else did he know?

"Leave the animals alone."

"Tell me where the stone is and I'll instruct my men to leave them in peace—instead of pieces."

Inwardly I swore. I never wanted the menagerie to pay the price for my involvement. It wasn't fair. But I already knew life wasn't fair. I learned that at a tender age when my mother told me I had to hide my true self for the rest of my life. I learned the lesson again the day she died and I was forced to live in the tunnels.

Maeron reached across the table and grabbed my hand, squeezing so hard I was afraid my bones would break.

"There is absolutely nothing to prevent me from taking you prisoner right now and torturing in the Tower until you confess. A charge of illegal magic would be no trouble at all to pin on someone like you."

I wrenched my hand away and dropped it to my lap. "You seem to forget that I have a relationship with more than just Callan. What would the king and queen say about arresting the knight who saved their daughter? What would Davina say?"

The mention of Davina's name triggered a tic in his cheek.

Gotcha.

"Davina need never know the truth of what happened, just as the West End Werewolf Pack will never know what truly became of Romeo."

"She adores you."

"And I adore her. She is the one bright spark in our miserable household."

How would he feel if he knew I was as much his sister as Davina was? I couldn't tell him, of course. The news that would save me would also condemn me to death. It was a no-win situation.

I stared at his face a beat too long, trying to identify any similarities between us. He didn't share our gray eyes. Maybe the straight nose and the plump upper lip.

"Lost in my eyes, Miss Hayes? And here I thought it was my brother you were interested in. Perhaps I misunderstood."

I raised my glass to my lips. "Just searching for evidence of humanity."

"I'm a vampire, Miss Hayes. Humanity is beneath us."

"Clearly."

"This is your last chance. You're either with me..."

I rolled my eyes. "Or against you. Yes, I've heard that one before." What was it with men and their inability to compromise?

"Well, Miss Hayes. Which one will it be?"

"Hmm. Let me think." I lit up. "I know."

He leaned forward, smug and eager. "Yes?"

I threw my glass of ale in his face. Turning invisible, I fled.

I passed through the doorway and ran like the wind. I knew every alley in this neighborhood. If Maeron wanted to track me, he'd have his work cut out for him.

Of course he knew I'd head to the flat and try to save the menagerie. As much as I wanted to go in person, I needed to escape the city before Maeron found me. That meant sending reinforcements.

I pulled out my phone and called Kami. "We have an emergency. I need everyone at the office."

"Everyone's already here except you. What's going on?"

My breathing grew ragged as I picked up the pace. "Vampires."

"A nest?"

"I'll explain when I get there." I whipped around a corner and came to a halt when I spotted two butterflies mid-air about twenty feet away. I backtracked and tried another route.

Barnaby appeared overhead. Bless that bird. I directed him to the flat to check on the others and report back. Then I called Mack. I hated to ask for a personal favor, but I needed someone to confirm whether Maeron's threat was real.

"You might want to bring backup," I said, once I'd made my request.

"What have you managed to get yourself into, London?"

"Maybe one of these days I'll be able to tell you the full story. Right now I need to make sure the animals are unharmed." According to Maeron, the ward was already broken so Mack would have no trouble getting inside.

"I'll report back as soon as I can."

I let myself exhale. "Thank you, Mack. You're the best."

Still running, I hung up. Thank the gods the stones were safe in my secret pocket dimension. Now if I could piece together the puzzle of my vision at the Atheneum, there was still a chance I could collect the remaining two stones before Maeron discovered their existence.

It was time to do the one thing I'd been avoiding—go to the Circus and enlist the aid of my supernatural monkeys.

10

The Knights of Boudica were headquartered in Piccadilly Circus in a building known as the Pavilion, which dated as far back as the 1850s. I quite liked the idea of an all-female group of badass knights working out of what was once a music hall and, later, a shopping arcade. We see your bandstand and we raise you one armory.

I tried to blow past Treena at the security desk, but she stopped me like any good security guard should.

"Trio's been looking for you," she informed me.

"How can you tell?"

"She sniffs everybody's boots and walks away the minute she realizes they don't belong to you."

"With six eyes you'd think she could tell without sniffing."

Treena gave me a sharp look. "Maybe she just likes the scent of dirty boots."

It was probably what Trio was used to. I'd encountered the three-headed beast living in a tunnel with her disagreeable master during an assignment and ended up adding her to the team at the Pavilion.

The building was quiet when I entered. It was the ideal moment to update the banner on the stone situation and ask for their help. If only I didn't feel sick to my stomach. Although I knew that asking for help wasn't a sign of weakness, I still would've preferred to handle this on my own. To keep my friends as far away from the danger zone as possible. But thanks to Maeron, there was now a clock ticking loudly in my ears.

I gathered my courage and clapped my hands together as I crossed the room to my desk. "I need everyone's attention, please. I have an announcement."

Kami glanced up from the paperwork on her desk. "You're marrying the vampire prince and living happily ever after?"

Briar rounded her desk and perched on the corner. "Does this mean we officially work for vampires now? Because I kind of like the niche we've established and I'm not sure that extending our services to vampires is the way to go."

"We're not extending our services to vampires," I said.

Trio hurried over at the sound of my voice and I rubbed all three heads in greeting.

One by one the other knights gathered around until everyone was accounted for.

"It's like story time," Kami said, wheeling her chair closer. "All we need is a burning corpse and a jug of ale to pass around."

Stevie Torrin opened the bottom drawer of her desk and produced a flask. "I got the ale covered."

Kami tapped her chin. "Now to find a burning corpse."

I took a deep breath and prepared to open the floodgates. "I need your help."

Six faces fixed on mine with burning curiosity. Seeing

their physical differences side by side conjured an image of the different species involved in Friseal's Temple. Kami's blond hair, creamy pink complexion, and stocky build. Stevie's brown skin with its silver undertones that now made me question whether she, too, had fae buried in her genetic history. Minka with her dark hair, bronze skin, and exceptional height, courtesy of an Asian father and a Nordic mother. Briar's wild red hair and heart of gold. Neera and Ione with their light brown hair and even features. Each was beautiful and strong in her own unique way.

I felt a rush of warmth as I prepared to unburden myself. My lips parted, spilling the secret of Friseal's Temple.

Stevie raised her chin a fraction. "Tell us what you need, London. We're your banner and we're here for you."

Although I knew they would, I still felt relieved to hear the words. "I need to recall my visions from the Atheneum in slow motion so I have time to study everything I saw."

Minka bit her lip. "And how do you propose we do that?"

I pointed to Kami. "I need your mind control magic." I shifted my finger to Minka. "And your spell expertise."

Minka shimmied in her seat. "I'm not sure I'd call it expertise."

"Only because you don't cast spells often enough," Neera said. "You'd be a first-class witch if you stopped hiding behind paperwork all the time."

Minka squared her shoulders. "I do not *hide*. I am the office manager."

"We could hire an office manager to give you more time in the field," Kami suggested.

Stevie let loose a shrill whistle. "Now's not the time for that conversation." She turned back to me. "Do you really believe the temple story is true?"

"The Atheneum contains fact not fiction." Like the fact

that my father was King Casek himself. That particular fact was on a need-to-know basis and nobody here needed to know. Not now and not ever.

"London's right," Ione chimed in. "Whatever the vision showed her is true."

"What's the rush?" Kami asked. "Can't you just make notes as you remember them?"

"I'm not the only one in search of the stones. Someone's been going out of their way to hide any information regarding the temple," I said.

Minka perked up. "Who?"

Time for another unwelcome bombshell. "Prince Maeron."

All the knights began talking at once.

"But I know I'm at least one step ahead and I plan to keep it that way," I said, loudly enough to cut through the din.

"We can't go up against Prince Maeron," Minka insisted.

"No one is going up against him. We're simply outmaneuvering him."

"We'd be accomplices." Minka looked to the other knights for support, but no one said anything.

Kami punched her hands onto her hips. "I'm game. How soon can we start?"

"How about right now?" I asked.

"I don't understand why you need Kami," Briar said.

Kami spared a glance over her shoulder for the redhead. "She'll need help guiding her brain to the right memories."

"And then keeping it there until I've seen what I need," I added.

"I've never done anything like this before." Minka began rummaging through her desk drawer as though she might stumble upon a set of instructions.

"It may fail, but as long as you don't kill me, you're forgiven," I told her.

"What if we erase your memory?" Minka asked. "You wouldn't forgive me then."

I shrugged. "I won't remember then, will I?"

Minka looked at Kami. "What do you think?"

"I think a member of our banner needs help and we should do whatever we can," Kami replied.

Minka drew a shaky breath. "I'll need to ask you to sign off on a release form."

Laughter burst from my chest. "You're putting on your bureaucratic hat now? Are you serious?"

She liberated a sheet of paper from the drawer and began scribbling. "I won't be held responsible if you end up in a coma."

"Who's going to complain?" I shot back. "Big Red? Herman?"

"No forms." Kami snatched away the pen and tossed it over her shoulder. Trio immediately ran to fetch it and brought it back to Minka.

"Good girl," Minka said, wrinkling her nose as she patted each of the three heads.

I leaned against the edge of the desk. "Listen, I'm not expecting perfection and I understand the risks. Can we please get on with it? The clock's ticking."

Neera nudged Minka's shoulder. "We'll stay here and offer moral support. If anything goes wrong, we'll pitch in and help."

"I'll be the one getting my hands dirty and steering her brain," Kami said. "If anyone should be nervous, it's me."

Minka offered a hesitant nod. "I'll do my best."

I had no doubt she would. Minka was a pain, but she

cared deeply about her work and I knew I could rely on her to be one hundred percent professional.

Ione appeared cradling an oversized book in her arms. The brown leather cover was worn along the edges.

"Where did you get my grimoire?" Minka demanded.

Ione placed it in front of Minka on the desk. "I took the liberty of skimming the options. There's a good prospect on page thirty-four."

Minka opened the book to the suggested page. She scanned the ingredient list and the instructions. Finally she glanced up at me. "I've never done this before."

I squeezed her arm. "With the banner as my witness, I absolve you of any harm that may come to me during this experiment."

She met my gaze. "I'll need help gathering some of these ingredients."

Ione and Neera bumped elbows in their haste to offer assistance.

Minka's phone rang and Stevie swooped in to answer it. "Knights of Boudica. Your problem is our problem."

Minka scowled. "That's not our motto," she hissed.

Stevie walked away with the phone to her ear.

Neera used her phone to snap a screenshot of the ingredient list. "Set up the room. Ione and I will be back shortly."

Stevie returned to the desk and handed over the phone. "Someone wanted to offer you an extended warranty on your car."

"Did you tell them I don't have a car?" Minka asked.

Trio barked and I turned toward the entrance to see Barnaby. The raven flew inside and landed on the edge of my desk. A sense of calm washed over me.

"The menagerie is okay?" I asked. It was impossible to disguise the hopeful note in my voice.

Barnaby cawed just as my phone buzzed. I snatched it to my ear.

"Mack?"

"All good," he said. "I mean, every inch of this place has been ransacked, but all the hearts are still beating."

His update was music to my ears.

"How many animals do you count?"

Mack counted out loud until he reached the number five. "Is that all of them?"

"Yes, thanks. Do me a favor and refill their bowls while you're there. Food's labeled in the pantry."

Mack grumbled as he disconnected the call.

It seemed Maeron was all bark and no bite, at least in this instance. Maybe he wasn't the monster he pretended to be.

Or maybe I only wanted that to be true because I knew he was my brother.

"I need to evacuate the menagerie," I announced.

Briar raised her hand. "You don't have to ask me twice."

"You can't go alone in case there are eyes on the building."

Stevie cracked her knuckles. "I'll go with her. I'm in a mood and I'd love to take my frustrations out on a nosy vampire."

"They work for Prince Maeron, don't forget. If they want to arrest you for any reason, they will."

Briar remained resolute. "They'd have to catch me first."

Now that I knew more about the different types of magic from Friseal's Temple, it occurred to me that Briar's inner monster might mean she was of mixed origin like me. A question for another time.

Kami looked at me, mistaking my contemplative expression for concern. "Don't worry. The animals will be fine."

"I'll never forgive myself if something happens to them." Or my friends.

She folded her arms. "How many times have you taken responsibility for stray animals?"

"I have no idea. Who can count that high?"

"And how many times have they been harmed because of you?"

My shoulders sagged. "Okay, I see your point."

"Do you think there's a chance Prince Maeron will send guards to arrest us here?" Minka asked.

"He didn't find what he wanted and he's shown his hand, so I definitely think he'll make another move soon."

"I can tell you're nervous," Kami said. "Why don't we discuss my bit while everybody else is prepping?"

I vacated the desk and accompanied Kami to the armory so we could talk in private. Trio followed.

"Want me to kick her out?" Kami asked.

I cut a glance at the three-headed dog. "She can stay."

Three tongues dropped down in unison to express gratitude.

Kami closed the door and faced me. "A lot can go wrong with this."

"I know, but if it goes right, it may be the break we need."

"What if the vampires figure out the location of the stones first?" Kami asked.

"They don't even know they exist yet." And that 'yet' was all the lead I needed. Whatever the books might've revealed about Friseal's Temple, it wasn't enough to direct Maeron to the other two stones.

"Tell me everything you remember about the vision," Kami said, "and I'll do my best to get you back there."

Half an hour later, I was on a single mattress in the

middle of a chalk circle on the floor of the armory. Five white candles surrounded me.

"Is the mattress really necessary?" I asked. It smelled like mildew, which made sense given that Neera had taken it from the janitorial closet in the Pavilion lobby.

"The more we can recreate a proper sleep environment, the better our chances of success," Minka explained.

I was convinced it was her idea of punishment for forcing her to participate.

"Minka, you take notes of anything I say in my sleep," I ordered. And I'd try like hell to remember the rest.

"I'm ready." Kami positioned herself on the edge of the mattress. In her hand was a bottle with bright purple potion that Minka had mixed with the ingredients.

Minka sat on a folding chair outside the circle. "Me too."

Kami thrust the bottle at me. "Drink up, Sleeping Beauty. See you on the other side."

I sniffed. "I smell lemon."

"Where on earth would we find a fruit as exotic as lemon?" Ione asked. "We're resourceful, but we're not that good."

I tipped back the bottle and drank. There was no taste of lemon, which was a shame. 'Vile' was the only description I could think of. I choked it down and tried to keep it from making a repeat appearance.

Kami took the empty bottle from me. "Sweet dreams."

I made myself as comfortable as possible on a stinking, lumpy mattress and closed my eyes. Once I was asleep, Kami would guide my mind to the vision I had in Wales and hold it there until I could note all the salient details. Hopefully there would be something in my mind's eye that could lead me to the stones or even the temple's original location.

My breathing deepened and eventually I slipped into

darkness. When I opened my eyes, I was in a familiar place but not the one I was expecting.

The guest tower at Peyton Castle where Princess Louise had sent assassins to kill me.

A shirtless Callan stood in front of me. Those intense green eyes reflected hunger and hope and my body instinctively shuddered in response. I hoped my reaction was only in the dream.

From the other side of the bed, Kami grinned at me. "This looks nice and cozy. Memory or fantasy?"

I crossed my arms and glared at her. "You're supposed to be guiding, not creeping."

"I'm not opposed to letting you have a little fun first." She observed Callan's muscular frame. "That is one royal physique. Too bad we don't like vampires, right?"

Callan reached for me, cupping the back of my head. My pulse sped up.

"Now, Kami," I insisted.

"Hang on tight," she said.

My head lurched and the view went black. No more Callan. I swept aside any feelings of disappointment. There were more important matters and Callan was a distraction I couldn't afford.

My eyes opened again but I saw nothing except an inky black void. I concentrated and the void began to take shape of a glossy black oval. No, not an oval. A shell.

I strained for a better look.

A black tortoise.

What did a tortoise have to do with the stones?

Tall trees came into view, unusually slender and straight. A rush of water fell from a cliff and washed the vision of the shell away. The black faded to gray until a new scene shimmered into view. I squinted, unaccustomed to the harsh light.

"Seabirds. Secluded beach. Sandstone cliffs," I murmured.

"You can see all that?" Kami's disembodied voice asked.

"Yes. It's light here." And stunning too.

"How is it light?"

"It's a vision, remember? This took place before the Eternal Night."

"Right. What else?" Kami prodded.

Waves crashed against the rocks below. I could be anywhere coastal.

"Any sign of life? A village or town?" Kami asked.

I surveyed the land. Nothing but nature as far as the eye could see. No smoke billowing from a chimney. I peered over the edge of the cliff to the water and was greeted to the sight of a black and white bird with an orange beak and matching orange feet on the ledge below.

"A puffin," I said, delighted.

The puffin sensed my presence and tilted his head to look at me.

"Are you certain it's a puffin?" Kami asked.

"Yes."

"That's helpful. Minka, write that down."

I couldn't hear Minka's response. Only Kami's voice permeated my dream.

"Start walking," Kami directed. "What else can you see?"

I ventured away from the cliffside and focused on the landscape.

I felt a rise of excitement when I spotted a formation in the distance. The upside of not being swaddled in darkness. "I see a ring of standing stones."

"Big deal. Standing stones are a dime a dozen."

"In Scotland they are," I corrected her.

Kami snorted. "Good luck roaming around House Duncan territory to find stones."

"I'm not going to roam. I'm going to keep looking right now." There had to be a distinguishable landmark somewhere.

A gust of wind disrupted my view. When I cleared the dust from my eyes, I seemed to be at a different spot. I didn't remember this from my vision. Then again, there'd been so much information crammed in my head at once, it was unsurprising I'd failed to fully process it all and nearly vomited.

In the distance I noticed a sea stack that was nearly as tall as the cliff behind it.

"There's a rock formation in the shape of a tower." My heart seized. "Kami, I recognize this."

"From your vision?"

"No, I mean recognize where I am."

The changing sky drew my attention away from the rocky tower. All around me the sky was awash in brilliant shades of pink and orange. Even the sea had taken on a pinkish hue. I'd never seen anything like it.

"What magic is this?" I whispered to myself.

But I knew exactly what it was.

I was witnessing a sunset. Not a photograph but a real sunset that occurred sometime deep in our history.

"I'm so glad we did this," I whispered. My brain hadn't registered any of this magnificence in Wales.

As the sun continued its descent, the colors began to fade. Soon I'd be plunged into darkness, the same as any normal day. A shiver ran through me as I tried to hold tight to the incredible view. I didn't want it to end.

"London, where are you?" Kami's voice interrupted my reverie.

I broke away from the setting sun and studied the rock tower once known as the Old Man of Hoy. No one in this world could see it anymore because it was bathed in perpetual darkness, but I'd seen it in enough books to remember.

"London!" Minka's voice cut through my hazy thoughts.

"Orkney," I said. "I need to go to Orkney." I sat up and opened my eyes, only to realize that Kami was shaking my arm.

"You need to go," Kami said. "Take the underground exit. We'll cover you."

The armory door shook as fists pounded on the reinforced steel. Loud voices demanded entry.

Maeron's men.

I jumped to my feet and Ione tossed me the axe.

I stared in awe. "When did you get Babe?"

"I swiped your bag from the office when the security alarm went off."

The metal on the armory door dented as the vampires continued to hit it.

Kami shoved me toward the entryway to the underground passage. "Go!"

Weapon in hand, I ran to the wall of weapons and activated the secret door. The section of wall slid aside and I hurried across the threshold just as the armory door was torn off the hinges. The secret door closed behind me and plunged me into the abyss.

11

I emerged from the underground passage on a neighboring street and turned myself invisible. Once I made sure the coast was clear, I boarded a bus to Camden. Usually I went to Camden to see my friend Lann because the dwarf handled most of my smithing needs, but today my need was of a different nature.

I departed the bus and walked two blocks until I reached the alleyway that led to the smithy. I stopped halfway there and pushed open the door to the broomstick shop.

A man with thick glasses peered down his nose at me from behind the counter. "Can I help you, miss?"

"I'd like your best broomstick, please."

His brow lifted. "No budget?"

I approached the counter and slapped a handful of bills on the counter. "The sky's the limit." Or it would be if I managed this transaction. Flying was illegal without a special license, but it was a risk I was willing to take. My main goal was to not get shot out of the sky as I passed over Hadrian's Wall on my way to Scotland.

The man smiled. "I believe I have just the broomstick for you."

I left the shop with a satisfied smile and the broomstick known as 'The Bullet' tucked under my arm. Phase One accomplished. Now for Phase Two: not dying.

Between them, Houses Lewis and Duncan employed thousands of witches and wizards to guard their borders. What made me think I was skilled enough to fly safely into enemy territory? At the very least, my presence would be detected. Wales was a different story. House Kane didn't have the same level of tension with House Lewis and the border was less secure as a result. The home of the Highland king was another matter entirely. I was about to fly straight from the frying pan into the fire.

I took off from a nearby park and gave myself time to get comfortable on the broomstick. Flying was a lost skill—one that would've been passed down from generation to generation before the Eternal Night. My mother never learned either. Over time broomsticks became a tool of criminals and underground activists. I was neither—until now.

En route to Hadrian's Wall, I gave myself time to develop a plan. What kind of magic would help me cross the border undetected? My multiplicity magic wouldn't be useful in this situation. My blood was capable of breaking and creating wards, but it couldn't cloak my presence. I'd be detected and immediately become a target on the ground in Scotland. Same with invisibility. They wouldn't see me with the naked eye, but they'd have magic that detected a flying object.

A glance ahead delivered my salvation. A flock of blackbirds flew north in V-formation. If I could nestle myself between them and draw them closer together, I could camouflage myself and ride straight into Scottish airspace without tipping off either House.

I increased the broomstick's speed to the point where the handle started to vibrate. I was pushing The Bullet's limits, but I had to catch up. These blackbirds were my best chance.

The birds at the back of the line squawked in protest as I attempted to join their flock. Ignoring them, I rode straight into the center of the V and tapped each of their tiny bird brains to win them over. I'd release them as soon as I was across the border and out of danger. The blackbirds huddled closer to me. Unfortunately I was too anxious about getting caught to enjoy the ride.

We passed over Hadrian's Wall and continued toward Scotland. Despite the peace treaty still in effect, House Lewis spent a great deal of money protecting the northern border from another House Duncan incursion. It was almost as though they didn't trust King Glendon. Go figure.

The blackbirds were so close that their feathers brushed against me from all sides. Good thing I wasn't ticklish or I'd die laughing.

The whole area was enshrouded in darkness which I assumed was another defensive measure. It wouldn't surprise me to learn that lights were banned by House Lewis this far north.

I wasn't sure of the exact moment I crossed into House Duncan territory. Orkney was at the very northern end of the country, though, so I still had a long way to go. The air already seemed crisper and smelled fresher. I was accustomed to the stench of Britannia City—so accustomed, in fact, that I barely noticed it until I was somewhere else.

Once I felt confident my entry was undetected, I released my hold on the birds. They dispersed, removing their soft feathery blanket and leaving me exposed. Not for the first time I silently thanked Minka for insisting on magical armor for the banner. It protected me against the elements as well as opponents.

The broomstick began to feel warm against my bare hands and the vibrations returned. I slowed my speed but it was too late. Smoke wafted from the broomstick. So much for the best brand. If I made it back to the city, I'd write a strongly worded letter to the manufacturer.

The heat radiated between my thighs which meant the stick was hot enough to permeate my suit. I didn't have long.

A river snaked along the ground below—my best option for an emergency landing.

I started to make my descent but it was too late. I crashed and burned. Literally. The broomstick split in two and caught fire. I plunged into the water holding a splinter of wood the size of a matchstick.

The current was relatively calm and I easily propelled myself to the surface. I dragged myself to the riverbank and hobbled to dry land. Directly in front of me stood the remains of a castle. My mother had told me that castles were a common feature of Scotland. I remembered asking her why King Glendon hadn't destroyed all the castles other than his own the way Queen Britannia had destroyed most of the churches. My mother had gazed at me in wonder.

You must get that from your father, she'd said. It was one of the few times she'd acknowledged his existence.

What? I'd asked.

She'd dropped her gaze. *Never mind.*

Did she think I'd inherited a monstrous side from King Casek? The realization was unsettling.

I returned my focus to the castle. Vines covered one side of the dilapidated structure. If the building was as abandoned as it looked, it would provide me with shelter and safety while I developed a plan to travel the rest of the way to Orkney. It would help to know where I landed.

I recovered two pieces of the broomstick that had landed on the ground and rubbed them together to create a small fire so I could use one as a torch. I approached the castle with caution. It was possible another creature used this shell as a refuge and I didn't want to engage in a turf war. If it was occupied, I'd simply move on.

I held up the makeshift torch and marveled at the fragments of medieval fortification mixed with nineteenth century construction. From what I could see, this building had been remade several times over until its eventual collapse.

To my great relief, there was no sign of life. I took a deep breath and entered. If only I knew where I was, I could try to identify the former castle and make my mother proud.

I passed through two large columns that were once connected by a wall. I couldn't tell whether the damage had been inflicted by soldiers, a beast, or the result of natural causes.

I continued to the banquet hall. It was a long room with what would've been a high ceiling if it weren't now open to the sky. A narrow table stood in the middle of the room with enough space for thirty guests, but only a single chair sat at its head. A bowl rested in the center of the table and I realized with a start it was filled with colorful fruit. I sniffed the sweet-scented air. *Fresh* fruit.

My gaze swept the room. It didn't take a genius to figure out that a single chair and a bowl of ripe fruit suggested this castle was occupied.

My heart squeezed at the sight of a plum nestled among the other fruits. I'd eaten a plum once when I was six. My mother had managed to snag one at Christmastime. She'd offered me the whole plum, of course, but I'd refused. We split it in half. I still recalled the deep purple juice that splattered on my arm as I bit into the fruit's soft flesh. We'd laughed and I'd licked the juice from my flesh so as not to waste it.

I leaned closer to see the other treasures in the bowl. There was a small orange. A cheerful pink apple. A heaven-scented lemon. No lime.

My mind immediately snapped back to Peyton Castle where Callan and I had danced among the lime trees. Limes had a way of revealing the truth and I'd been fortunate to escape that encounter with the vampire prince without spilling my secrets. It was, more importantly, the night we kissed and I'd forever associate limes with the Lord of Shadows.

I resisted the urge to pluck the plum from the bosom of the bowl. Instead I advanced, curious to see what other items of interest the castle contained.

As I reached the threshold of the adjacent room, a half dozen blackbirds burst from their hiding spot and took to the skies. My heart hammered in my chest and I stood with my back to the wall while I caught my breath. I'd been too distracted to sense the birds. I couldn't let that happen again. Staying alert could mean the difference between life and death.

Although the birds were gone, I felt a lingering presence.

"Hello?" I raised the torch higher to illuminate the room ahead.

"They are my creatures and this is my castle." An ethereal woman floated toward me. She wore her golden hair loose around her shoulders. Her pale, unblemished skin radiated youth. To say she was beautiful...Even if she weren't hovering inches off the ground, she'd still appear otherworldly.

"I apologize. I didn't realize anyone lived here. I was only seeking shelter on my way to Orkney."

"Then you are well on your way. Follow the river north and it will lead you there."

"Thank you. Again, I apologize for the intrusion." I turned to leave, but a strong wind blew me back against the wall and pinned me in place.

"You will go when I say so." The ghost hovered a few inches off the floor and her eyes blazed with unexpressed fury.

"I meant no disrespect by entering your home uninvited. I'm more than happy to leave you in peace."

She ignored my words. "You're a witch."

"Yes."

"But your magic is…different." She cocked her head and examined me. "Why do you wear such strange clothing?"

"I'm a knight."

She laughed lightly. "Knights are valiant men in silver armor who slay dragons."

"I try to avoid slaying dragons. Usually they're just misunderstood." I connected with my magic and pushed against the will of the ghost. I felt her hold on me snap and took a step forward.

The ghost regarded me. "You're not like any witch I've ever met."

I rolled my neck from side to side. "We're all special in our own way. My name is London."

"Enyd. I was once flesh and bone like you." Her gaze raked over me. "Although my beauty far surpassed that of other mortal women."

I resisted the urge to smile. "I can see that."

"It's been many years since I've had a visitor. If you promise to sit with me for a spell, I'll let you—"

I couldn't tell whether she said "live" or "leave." Either way it seemed wise to agree. "I'll stay."

The ghost floated across the room. "You must be tired after your journey. Rest your weary feet at the banquet table."

I followed her to the long table and she motioned to the chair. "You said those birds were your creatures. Do you have any other creatures around the castle?" Preferably one that could get me to Orkney faster.

"Only the birds dwell in the castle with me, although the river is home to many creatures."

"Yes, but which ones won't kill me?" My back ached as I eased it against the slat of the chair. Staying upright on the broomstick had used more muscles than I realized. I'd be sore tomorrow.

"The river is flush with a variety of fish. I've even seen dolphins."

River dolphins. Now there was a possibility. I tucked the idea in the corner of my mind and focused on my hostess. The sooner I played nice, the sooner I could leave.

"Tell me, Enyd. How does a beauty like you end up in a dump like this?"

"Men, naturally." Enyd twirled. Her hair swirled around her head like a web of golden silk.

Naturally.

The ghost stretched her translucent body across the table and tipped her head back to address me. "I was an only child—a dreaded daughter—and my father longed to find me a suitor, but none was forthcoming."

"Why not?"

"We had nothing to offer. My father was convinced my

beauty would be enough to persuade a powerful landowner." She sighed dramatically. "He was wrong. Finally he left me for dead. There wasn't enough food and I was expendable."

"That's awful. I'm sorry that happened to you."

She flipped to her front and rested her elbows on the table, kicking her legs behind her like a carefree schoolgirl. "A man came to me in the darkness and offered assistance. He said his name was Erasmus. Having no other options, I accepted and he brought me to his castle to live. His only requirement was that I never subjected him to the light. This was before the Eternal Night, of course. He kept the castle shrouded in darkness at all times as a security measure. Thieves were rampant in the region and he was often away. I quickly fell in love with his gentle spirit and told him I didn't care whether he was fair. I would love him all the same." She gazed wistfully at the great outdoors beyond the crumbling wall. "Erasmus refused. He traveled frequently and permitted me to invite neighboring women to join me so I wouldn't be lonely. He was a considerate man."

I could see how it might have been difficult for her to live in a desolate area in complete darkness with only occasional visits from her lover. The skeptical part of me wondered whether he kept another family and only wanted to conceal his face in order to hide his true identity.

"How did he cloak the castle?"

"He told me he hired a wizard to create a spell that kept his home in perpetual darkness." She averted her gaze. "I laughed at the time. I didn't believe in magic. I thought they were nothing more than fairytales."

"How did you explain the darkness?"

"I thought it was the castle's location. That he'd been

shrewd in his choice of placement. I recognize now that was naive, but you must remember I was only sixteen when we met and had very little experience in the world. I went straight from my father's home to the castle."

"At least you found happiness."

Her voice trembled slightly. "For a time. Then one day the women and I were chatting in the garden and they began to question me about Erasmus. They said his frequent absences were strange and that they were as likely as we were to be targeted by thieves, yet they didn't feel the need to keep their homes hidden."

"And you began to doubt him?"

She nodded. Her eyes glistened with sadness and I felt a rush of sympathy for her. Hers was clearly not a story with a happy ending.

"The women said he must be a horrible monster and that was the real reason he didn't wish me to glimpse his true form. They put ideas in my head—one suggested that he left to ravage the countryside and only returned when his thirst for blood had been quenched."

"I take it you gave in to temptation?"

She sniffed. "One night when he returned home after a long absence, I gathered my courage and lit a candle at his bedside while he slept. By the gods, he was magnificent in every way." Shuddering, she drew herself into a seated position on the table. "Then he awoke."

I swallowed hard. "Was he angry?"

"Worse. He was crushed that I failed to trust him. Then I saw his fangs."

Ah. "You didn't know about vampires?"

Enyd shook her head. "I believed the women were right. That I'd been taken by a monster. I was terrified and ran screaming from the bedroom." She hugged herself. "I was such a fool. He showed me love and kindness and I rewarded him with betrayal."

I couldn't help but think of Callan. Once upon a time, the vampire prince had terrified me, but that was down to his species and reputation rather than how he treated me. Maybe a vampire who treated me with kindness and respect and was secretly working to mass produce synthetic blood deserved the benefit of the doubt.

Enyd eyed me closely. "You view me as the monster, don't you?"

"No, definitely not. You were young and frightened, and he lied to you." A lie by omission was still a lie. I knew this all too well. "What happened next? Did he come back?"

"Every day I watched and waited for his return." She shifted to an upright position. "One day a man arrived on horseback. I recognized him as the husband of one of our neighbors. He carried the head of Erasmus on a spike and tossed it at my feet. 'We have slain your monster,' he told me." Tears streamed down her cheeks. "I dropped to my knees and begged him to kill me."

"Is that what happened to you?" A violent death like that could explain her attachment to the earthly plane.

"The man refused to strike me. I grabbed his blade and the metal burned my hand." She held up a flat palm, although I couldn't see any marks on its unblemished surface.

I blinked. "You weren't human."

She shook her head. "I didn't know until that moment. I plunged the blade into my chest and killed myself."

I winced at the image in my head. "Do you think your parents knew?"

"I suspect my mother did. Impossible to say for certain though."

"Do you think Erasmus sensed that about you? Maybe that's why he was drawn to you?"

She clasped her hands in front of her. "I've often asked myself that very question. Perhaps it wasn't me he loved. Perhaps it was something specific about me that he didn't even register on a conscious level."

"And you know nothing about your history? Even in death?"

"Sadly, no. Not all secrets are revealed once you shuffle off your mortal coil."

"I think you have fae blood," I told her.

"The fae are nothing but a myth."

"That's what you thought about vampires, too, remember?" I wasn't judging her. I'd had the same reaction.

She twisted toward the fruit bowl. "I wonder if that's how I manage to enchant the fruit. I assumed it was the power of the dead."

"Have you tried to move on?"

Enyd frowned. "Why would I want to move on? This castle is where I spent the only happy days of my life."

"Exactly. Your life." Which had been over for quite some time.

She pressed her lips together. "I take your point."

"Have you considered letting go? That maybe there's a chance you'd be reunited with Erasmus in the afterlife?"

She scoffed. "You don't truly believe that, do you?"

I wasn't sure. I liked the idea of seeing my mother again someday. I liked the idea of hope.

"I would rather try for a future than cling to a past that no longer serves me."

Enyd nodded toward the bowl. "A gift for you. Take whichever one pleases you."

My gaze flicked to the ripe plum. "Any one?"

"I can tell you've already made your selection. Take it. It's yours."

I inhaled its ripe scent before sliding it into my pocket.

"Surely you'd prefer to eat it now." Her lips melted into a smile that didn't quite reach her sharp eyes.

"No, thank you. I'd prefer to savor it."

Her smile widened encouragingly. "Just one bite. I'd like to watch you enjoy it. It's been so long since I've tasted food. Allow me to live vicariously through you."

"I think it makes more sense to preserve it for emergencies."

In truth I wanted to keep it until the enchantment wore off and it turned to rot, if only to extend the feeling of closeness to my mother. The plum served as a bridge to the past and I intended to stand in the middle until it crumbled beneath my feet.

Languidly she rose to her full frame. If I'd only focused on her body movements, I would've missed the intensity of her stare. Her eyes simmered with resentment and something else. It took me a moment to identify the something else, but I got there in the end. I'd encountered enough vampires in my thirty years to recognize the look.

Hunger.

"I can sense your need," she said. "Why resist it?"

And I sensed hers. My hand slid over the lump in my pocket. I didn't know what would happen when I bit into that plum, but I had no intention of finding out.

I vacated the chair and took a step backward. "I appreciate your hospitality, Enyd, and I wish you well…"

"Please don't go. I've so enjoyed your company."

I backed away slowly. "I've taken up enough of your time."

She trailed after me. "Don't you see? That's the problem. I have nothing *but* time."

"Unfortunately I have the opposite problem."

"Don't leave me!" she wailed.

I inched toward the exit. "Let go, Enyd. Don't hold yourself captive anymore."

"Do you think I haven't tried to leave? That bastard with the sword cursed me!"

And there it was. The truth. Enyd wasn't tethered to this castle because of some true love fairy tale. Her spirit had been cursed.

"Was Erasmus even a vampire?" I asked.

Another step backward.

"Of course. All of that is true." She paused. "Except I'm the one who put his head on a spike."

I didn't see that coming. Neither did Erasmus, apparently. "I thought you loved him."

"*He lied to me*. No one lies to me and escapes punishment. My father was the first to learn that lesson."

I shivered. Even in her ethereal form, her rage was palpable.

"He lied to you, too?"

"He told me he'd found me a suitor and then left me for dead." She tossed her golden hair over her shoulder. "I found him before he could return home."

"Who's the man that cursed you?"

"The family of Erasmus discovered my treachery and hired a wizard to find me and curse me."

"What's the curse?" I didn't really care. I only wanted to distract her while I continued my path to the exit. I had no clue how to kill a cursed ghost and no time to find out.

"I remain trapped in these ruins, suffering from the

sensation of starvation and left with a bowl of fruit I cannot eat."

"What happens if you try to eat?"

"The only time I'm able to make contact is when a living creature takes the first bite." Her lips curved into a treacherous smile. "Then I'm free to devour them both."

"Sorry to disappoint you, but I'm not on the menu."

"Trust me, pet. I have ways of persuading you." She whistled and the flock of blackbirds returned. They perched along the uneven wall of the castle and awaited their mistress's command.

I reached for their minds and was relieved to find them pliable.

Enyd motioned to the birds. "My friends are more than happy to convince you."

I held on to their tiny minds and asserted my will. One by one they vacated the perch and dive-bombed the apparitional beauty. Although they couldn't hurt her, they could distract her long enough for me to make my escape.

Enyd shrieked and lurched forward. The blackbirds continued to make loops through her and around her. No weapon would harm her and I wasn't sure which magic might be effective, so I chose the only option available to me.

I turned and fled.

I crossed the threshold and the castle walls started to shake. I narrowly avoided the falling stones. The last thing I needed was to get knocked unconscious. I'd end up as a smorgasbord for a psychotic ghost.

I dodged a wooden beam that landed on the ground in front of me and split in two.

"Throw me the plum, I beg you."

I craned my neck to see Enyd standing on the other side

of the doorway. Her arms were outstretched and her beautiful face was contorted.

By running away with the plum, I'd triggered whatever failsafe the witch had created. Most likely it prevented the fruit from leaving the castle since it was somehow tied to Enyd.

"Throw me the plum!" Her screech pierced my ears.

I turned to face her. "Consider it a gift." It was a kindness to set her free, although I was sure the malevolent spirit didn't see it that way.

Stones shook and tumbled until they blocked her path. It seemed this was one solid object she couldn't pass through. I continued to watch as the remains of the castle collapsed. Dirt sprayed in the air and I jumped backward to avoid the fall of a column. The earth opened and swallowed the remnants of the castle whole. Enyd's screams filled the air and I winced at the primal sound. Pain was pain, whether it was deserved or not.

Suddenly the air fell silent. No more screams or falling stones. Only when the dust settled and I saw there was nothing left did I turn and walk away.

12

I stood at the river's edge and scanned the minds within range. Too small. Too weak. Too resistant.

Bingo.

A pod of dolphins appeared downstream, their dorsal fins rising and falling beneath the surface in quick succession. I'd never hitched a ride from dolphins before. There was a first time for everything.

I turned to see whether there was anything I could use and was pleased to see vines strewn across the ground that were left behind by the castle. I grabbed the longest vine I could find and returned to the bank.

Coaxing the pod toward me, I waded into the water. I tied the vine around the front dolphin's body and held on to the end. Then I planted each foot on a dolphin and urged them forward.

I wasn't sure what the proper command was in this situation. I mean, who water skied on dolphins?

"Mush," I called.

The dolphins started to swim. I remained in an upright position and rode them all the way to where the North Sea and Atlantic Ocean met. My face was drenched from the spray, but it didn't detract from my enjoyment.

Up ahead, the archipelago of Orkney awaited me. I'd never traveled this far north. From what I could discern through the sheet of darkness, the landscape was as stunning today as it was centuries ago. The countryside of Devon had been a stark contrast to Britannia City, but Orkney was on a different level entirely. It seemed to me that the sun's presence was stronger here, as though I could feel it straining to push through the layer of volcanic ash and bathe us all in its golden light.

Once on land, I squinted to see rocky terrain, not that I expected flat and sandy beaches. If only my mother could see me now. She would've been an explorer if she'd had the freedom to travel. So many people were denied their full potential thanks to the Eternal Night and vampire rule. Then again, maybe vampires felt the same way back when they were still forced to live in the shadows. I pictured an exuberant Davina shoved back into hiding, her flame of enthusiasm doused by disagreeable circumstances. I knew what that felt like and I didn't wish it on anyone else.

I had to find the waterfall from my vision. My stomach rumbled and I thought of the ripe plum still in my pocket.

No. That plum was like having my mother with me. I'd only eat it if my options ran out and I was going to starve to death. I hadn't reached that point.

I remembered seeing tall and slender trees in my dream so I advanced toward the only trees in view. My leg muscles ached from my dolphin ride, but I soldiered on.

I didn't pass another living soul on my way to the trees. I started to feel a low hum deep in my core and moved in the direction of the sound. The vibration grew stronger and I followed the sensation until I arrived at a familiar place.

The waterfall from the vision.

I surveyed the shadows watching for any sign of life. There was no birdsong here. No woodland creatures scuttling along the ground. The vibration ceased and the only sound was the rushing of the water as it poured into a clear blue pool below. If I had to spend time here while I figured out next steps, this wasn't a bad place to do it.

A gentle breeze tickled my nose. Somewhere in the distance an owl hooted.

It was even darker here than in the city tunnels. I explored the area, checking for symbols or significant stones.

Nothing.

I shifted to my bottom to give my legs a rest. I was powerful but that didn't mean I was impervious to cramps. I would've made a terrible scout. Briar was better suited for those tasks. She was quiet, patient, and not prone to fidgeting. I blamed my magic. I had to fidget or my magic would explode—or so I told myself. More likely I simply disliked sitting still.

At the thought of magic, my skin began to cast a silver glow in the darkness. Terrific. It was like getting your period unexpectedly in white pants, except worse because I could actually die of something other than embarrassment.

I let the silver filter through my skin. It was helpful to shed a bit of light on the area and the odds of anyone happening by were slim to none.

It didn't seem like a coincidence that fae had glowed with a silver light. Was it that drop of fae blood in our ancestry that made a dhampir so powerful? Was chaos magic only expressed through our rare genetic line? What if, all this time, vampires had been executing half vampires that wouldn't have had any special power at all? It was bad enough to outlaw an entire species, but knowing there was a chance they posed no threat to vampires made the whole affair even more sickening than before.

Another breeze blew past, rustling through the trees. A patch of black moved into my line of sight. It was darker than the shadows that surrounded it. Midnight on the move.

My eyes adjusted to see an oval silhouette and the black tortoise from my dream wandered into view. Not only was the creature real but also in the here and now. How old could the tortoise possibly be?

The creature ambled toward the pool of water. I wondered whether the silver glow had drawn the tortoise in my direction. It was possible the tortoise felt a primal connection to my ancient magic.

I shifted back to my haunches and watched to see what the tortoise would do next. He was unusually large. His shell was the size of a six-person oval dining table. He reached the edge of the pool and stretched his neck until his mouth met the water.

What was the protocol? Did I let him drink first and then pounce with my questions? He was a tortoise. How fast could he get away?

I continued to observe him from the shadows.

Once he finished drinking, he turned to regard me. "Are you simply here to observe or do you intend to learn something?"

His voice startled me. I wasn't expecting a talking tortoise and I certainly wasn't expecting one that sounded like a grumpy uncle demanding that someone pass the gravy at the annual Christmas dinner.

I nearly tripped over my own feet in my hurry to get to him. That would've been an elegant introduction.

When I got within a foot of the tortoise, I realized I had

no idea how to greet him. Was he some kind of ancient deity? Did I bow? He'd managed to survive multiple Great Eruptions and the rise and fall of mighty civilizations. It seemed to me he'd earned a little respect.

The tortoise crawled closer. "I recognize you."

My brows drew together. "You've seen me before?"

"Not your physical form. Your essence." He gave me an appraising look. "I recognize the magic within you."

"I'm glad one of us does."

I felt unexpectedly nervous. This tortoise might possess immense power. The kind of power that could obliterate me from existence and no one would ever know what became of me.

Then again, he seemed like more of a gentle giant.

I lowered myself to his height.

"Don't be absurd. Use those long legs the gods gave you." He lifted his stubby front leg. "Some of us haven't been as blessed."

"You seem to have done okay for yourself. Not many creatures can say they've been around since the dawn of time."

"You just called me old."

"It's a compliment."

"Hmm. As long as you don't refer to me as a turtle, you and I can be friends. Now, tell me why you've come."

"I glimpsed your shell in a vision, although I wasn't sure exactly what I saw until now."

He nodded approvingly. "As it should be. If I were easy to find, I would've been dead long ago."

My gaze swept the waterfall and the protective trees. "Is this the place where Friseal built his tower?"

"The wizard believed he had the best chance of reaching the heavens from here."

"Because it's so far north?"

"Because it's so beautiful."

I glanced around helplessly. "So do I just ask you my questions about the stones and you answer them?"

"Do I look like a librarian to you? Consult the pool. That's where you'll find your answers."

I shifted to my knees and lowered my face to the water. Despite the darkness, it was clear enough to see the bottom. I suspected the water was much deeper than it appeared.

The tortoise rammed his shell against my butt and knocked me into the water. As I plunged into the pool, I opened my eyes to identify the surface. I knew it was easy to get confused in dark water and swim in the wrong direction. My mother had taught me to look for the bubbles and follow them to the top.

There was no need though. The pool was even clearer underwater. I glanced upward and saw the tortoise peering down at me. As I kicked my feet to propel myself toward him, a thick fog engulfed me. It was so dense that I felt separate from the rest of the world. I tried to swim through the fog and realized I was no longer in water but on land. I forced my way through the fog and there it was.

The Spirit Stone.

I recognized its markings from the vision. But how? Where was I?

I tried to focus on the surrounding area to see whether any features stood out. There was no Kami or Minka to help me remember.

I saw a rugged landscape and a dramatic cliff overlooking the sea. I needed more. I focused on the trees instead of the forest and it was then that I saw it. A large slab of gray rock with words chiseled into its belly.

I squinted to read the letters.

Eilean a' Cheò.

I smiled, recognizing the Norsk name for 'Isle of Mist' and once again said a silent thank you to my mother for filling me with more knowledge than I ever thought necessary.

The fourth stone was on the Isle of Skye.

I waited a few minutes to see whether the pool revealed the location of the fifth and final stone, but the fog turned back to water and I saw the face of the tortoise staring down at me once again.

I swam to the surface and climbed out of the pool to sit beside the tortoise.

"You're welcome," he said.

"You could've warned me before you knocked me in."

"It's a lonely life I lead. I have to get my chuckles somewhere."

I squeezed the excess water from my hair. "I found the fourth stone. What about the fifth one?"

The tortoise snorted. "This is the trouble with youth today. You expect to be spoon-fed everything."

I ignored the jibe. "You won't tell me?"

"Not a chance."

"Even if it means that the stone could end up in the wrong hands?"

The tortoise's gaze settled on me for a long, uncomfortable moment. "And who are we to say whose hands are right and whose are wrong?"

I angled my head to the water. "So this isn't a King Arthur and Excalibur situation? There's no worthiness requirement in order to control the stones?"

"Control is an illusion. Someone might possess the stone, but they don't control it."

"Why do you hang around this pool if you already know all the information?"

"Because I'm thirsty."

I cracked a smile. "For knowledge?"

The tortoise looked me in the eye. "I'd tell you, but then I'd have to kill you."

"Fine. Keep your secrets. I have quite enough of my own."

"I agree. And you use them as a shield."

I frowned. "I have to protect myself and those I care about."

"You've grown comfortable on your island. You lean on your secrets the way an injured man leans on his cane."

"That's what allows him to walk."

The tortoise looked at me with weary eyes. "You're missing the point. You're not injured."

"You realize I'd be a walking target if I shared my secret?" And so would my friends. "I could lose my life."

"Seems to me you've lost much of your life anyway. Not letting anyone know the real you has a similar effect."

I brushed the dirt from my legs. "I guess you've had plenty of time to earn that advanced psychology degree."

"I've had a plenty of time to contemplate all that is and all that ever will be."

"A transcendental tortoise. Sounds about right."

"You need to trust."

"I do trust. I'm trying to protect them—and me. My mother trained me to survive."

"I fear she might have overemphasized your need to be alone in order to survive."

I rested my head against an obliging tree trunk. "You're alone. Isn't that how you've managed it for so long?"

"Just because you see me alone now doesn't mean I

spend all my time this way. I wouldn't have made it this far without the support of others."

"Is this your no-man-is-an-island speech?" I resumed a standing position. "I have friends. I'm far from alone."

"But you refuse to share your burden."

"It's bad enough I got them involved with Maeron. I would put my entire banner in danger if I told them about me." The king. My species. My power. The list went on and on.

"You put your entire banner in danger the moment you joined their ranks. Knowledge protects better than any secret ever could."

I was all finished with my therapy session. I needed to get to that stone before anyone else.

"I know the Spirit Stone is on the Isle of Skye, but I don't know exactly where." If I recalled correctly, the island was 600 square miles. That was still a lot of haystack in which to find my needle.

The tortoise took a slow, stubby step backward. "Use the Force, Luke."

My eyebrows inched up. "Did you seriously just Yoda me?"

His lipless mouth stretched into a smile. "You understand the reference? I knew I liked you."

"Some pop culture managed to survive the Great Eruption."

"An excellent franchise with a few hiccups we won't discuss since I'd like us to part as friends. If I didn't know any better, I'd believe I was the inspiration for that character."

"They would've had to know of your existence back then." And I seriously doubted it. We were all mere fantasies to the humans living prior to the Great Eruption.

"A tortoise can dream."

"You know, Yoda spends time teaching and training Luke. I traveled all this way. Can't you just tell me where the stone is?"

He shook his head in a sluggish fashion. "You can lead a horse to water, but you can't make her drink." He rotated counterclockwise. I decided his slow speed was to prevent him from losing his balance and tipping over. "It was nice to meet you. Best of luck with your quest."

"Aren't you supposed to say 'may the Force be with you?'"

He chuckled. "The Force is always with you."

It seemed incredible he'd managed to survive all these years moving at such a reduced rate. If a predator was ever in the mood for tortoise soup, he was a goner.

"Can you at least tell me if there's a shortcut to the Isle of Skye? The clock is ticking and..."

The tortoise kicked out a back leg and knocked me into the pool of water. Again.

My first instinct was to swim back to the surface, but I took a moment to consider his actions. He didn't just knock me in for fun the first time. He wanted to teach me a lesson.

I decided to learn.

I pivoted and swam through the water. Connecting to my magic, I concentrated on my desired location. I pictured the same rugged landscape that the water had shown me and willed the water to take me there.

With each stroke, I began to feel more certain that the pool acted as a portal. It would explain the tortoise's ability to travel widely and escape danger. It would also explain Friseal's ability to undertake such an ambitious project without raising any alarm bells. His discovery of the portal may have been the reason he chose this location for the tower.

I swam until my arms and legs ached and I was relieved to see sparks of light ahead. They were like underwater fireflies or will o' the wisps. I headed toward them and hoped I was on the right track. They gathered above my head and I bolted upward, breaking the water's surface.

The good news was that I was right about the portal. There was no sign of the waterfall or the pool. The bad news was that I seemed to have emerged too soon, like getting off at the wrong train stop. My head bobbed in a river about eight feet wide that stretched long in either direction.

Even worse, I'd emerged in front of a roving stable of kelpies. I counted six of them. Their broad black bodies glistened in the murky water and their manes writhed with slender serpents. They seemed to have been in pursuit of a river dolphin that swam straight past me. I was pretty sure the creature wished me luck as it escaped. The kelpies took one look at me and their nostrils flared in unison.

Shit.

"You don't want me," I said. "Trust me, there's very little meat on these bones."

They charged.

Cursing the portal's unfortunate timing, I swam for my life.

Teeth clamped around my ankle and bit. Hard.

I suppressed a scream. No one would hear me underwater anyway except more creatures eager for their next meal. I'd have to resort to magic and hope it didn't act as a beacon for others to find me.

Fat chance.

I focused on the water and used my elemental magic to give it a firm push. It was powerful enough to dislodge my ankle. I used their momentary confusion to my advantage and propelled myself up to the surface for air. I was close to the riverbank. If I could reach it in time...

Another jaw clamped on my foot. I fought the current and reached in vain for the reeds along the shoreline.

Strong fingers curled around my wrist and lifted me into the air. I dangled like bait above the river as the kelpies charged and splashed below me, angry to be deprived of another meal.

I was relieved to be pulled to safety. With a grateful smile at the ready, I spun to face my rescuer. My heart stopped.

"You've got to be kidding me."

13

I couldn't believe my eyes. The vampire prince had to be a mirage.

Callan looked at me as though he'd stumbled upon a rose in the desert. "You're alive."

"You thought I was dead?"

He answered by pulling me to land and gathering me in his arms. "I had to be sure." He cupped my cheeks in his hands and fastened his lips to mine. The kiss deepened and I melted against him, happy to be alive to experience this moment.

I could've stood with our bodies entwined all day, but unfortunately I had questions. Reluctantly I broke off the kiss. "How did you know where to find me?"

"I called in a favor from an old friend."

"An old friend with impressive tracking magic," I mused.

"Yes." His tone made it clear he intended to offer no further information on the subject.

I shook my head and tiny droplets sprayed from my hair. Once again, the magical armor was dry. When I got back to the Circus, I was going to buy Minka a pastry from that delicious place in Covent Garden. She'd earned it.

"Does anyone know you're here?" I asked.

"Aside from my friends, no. I couldn't risk it."

Now it was 'friends' plural. Hmm.

"There are things I need to tell you." He cast a furtive glance around us. "But not now. When I found out you were here, I wanted to throttle you, but that meant finding you first."

"Who told you?" So I knew which knight to blame when I got home.

"Kamikaze."

I swore. I couldn't believe my best friend was the one who ratted me out. My money had been on Minka.

"Is she okay? Is my banner okay?" Did he know about Maeron's men trying to break into the armory?

Callan nodded. "My brother blew off the incident as a bureaucratic misunderstanding."

"Do you believe him?"

"It's Maeron," he said, as though that answered the question.

Worry gnawed at my stomach. "Does he know where I am and that you came after me?"

Callan's brow creased. "What does he want with you? He knows you don't have the stone. Romeo told him so."

I longed to tell him everything—not just about Maeron, but about the stones and my father too.

But I couldn't. There was too much at stake. Callan's loyalty was to House Lewis, not to me. Just because he liked to kiss me, that didn't mean he'd be willing to go against both his royal families and support me.

It was a chance I couldn't take.

"I don't know," I said, and a small part of me died inside.

I wasn't sure why it pained me so much to lie to him. I'd been lying for so long, it was second nature to me.

You've grown comfortable on your island. You lean on your secrets the way an injured man leans on his cane.

Damn tortoise and his wise words.

Callan inched closer. His jaw looked ready to snap an oak tree in half. "Did my brother try to hurt you?"

"I didn't give him the chance."

Callan's snarl made the hairs on the back of my neck stand on end. "I'll kill the bastard. I'll pluck each hair from every inch of his body and then I'll personally draw and quarter him."

I clasped his hands in mine. "No, you won't." My voice was quiet but firm.

"Why not?"

"Because he's your brother and, for all his faults, you love him."

Callan opened his mouth to object but quickly closed it again. "He had no right."

"Maeron is playing his own game right now. I wandered onto the board." I shrugged. "I'm still here though."

"Thank the devil for that." He wrapped his arms around me and pulled me close. "I would never forgive myself if anything happened to you. Why did you need to come here? I thought you got what you needed in Wales."

"What makes you think the two trips are related?"

His mouth twitched. "Clandestine travel on your own. That's not the way of your banner. I don't even want to know how you got across the border this time."

My stomach growled.

"Never mind my questions. Let's get you something to eat. I don't know how you can focus on anything when you're hungry." He guided me away from the river.

"Where are we going?" There were no visible lights in the area.

"You'll see."

We arrived at a large oak tree to find a bay-colored horse with white flash tethered there.

"Where did you get a Clydesdale?"

"My favor involved transport as well as information."

When the horse noticed Callan, he snorted and tried to back away.

I laughed. "You make friends wherever you go, don't you?"

"He tolerates me. I promised him our time together would be short." He held out a hand to give me a boost. It was a gallant albeit unnecessary gesture.

I climbed on the horse's back. I caught a whiff of clove as Callan settled behind me. My body warmed when he snaked his arms around my waist and leaned his chest against my back.

"How far?" I asked.

"Their sanctuary is less than an hour from here as the crow flies."

Or as the horse trots. I craned my neck to look at him. "Who is 'they?'"

"My friends."

"I thought you were keeping their identity a secret."

"I didn't want to discuss it by the riverside. There are eyes and ears everywhere. Easier to divulge information in transit."

"Okay, we're in transit. Who are your friends?"

"They're called the Daughters of Persephone."

The name didn't ring any bells. "They're a group in Scotland?"

As he nodded, his cheek brushed against mine. "Years

ago my mother saved the life of one of them and they became friends. The Shades became like extended family to me."

"Shades?"

"That's what they call their members."

"Let me guess. They want a return to sunlight." Which made for an unlikely friendship with vampires. Not that I was one to talk.

"A reasonable guess, but actually they're witches with a vampire kink."

"Why Persephone? Hades wasn't a vampire."

"Close enough."

I leaned forward to nuzzle the horse's mane. I sensed a gentle yet tough disposition. A nice combination.

"Is it wrong to be jealous of a horse?"

I laughed. "Well, let's just say you're sitting at the right end for a statement like that."

The horse picked up speed as we arrived at flatter terrain. It was hard to see through the wall of darkness, but I could make out the silhouette of rolling hills around us. I took the opportunity to rest, although riding a horse did nothing to soothe my already-sore thigh muscles.

We rode in companionable silence for most of the way and I was reminded of our time in Devon. It seemed incredible that a vampire known as the Highland Reckoning was a calming presence for me, yet there was no denying he was.

A speck of light appeared on the horizon, so faint it was almost imperceptible.

"Almost there," Callan whispered in my ear. His lips brushed against my earlobe and I fought the urge to shiver.

"If they're so into vampires, why do they need a sanctuary?"

"It isn't for them."

The Clydesdale stopped between two sturdy oak trees. We were still swimming in a sea of darkness and the light seemed just as far away as it had twenty minutes ago.

"Why are we stopping?"

Callan climbed to the ground. "Because we're here."

The horse whinnied as though grateful to be rid of Callan. Tough to be tied to the Daughters of Persephone if you weren't a fan of vampires.

I patted the Clydesdale's side. "I understand, buddy."

The horse melted into the void.

Callan held my hand. It felt warm and powerful and pretty darn perfect. When did I get so soft?

"Ready?" he asked.

"For what?"

He tugged me forward and we stepped into the murk.

Fragments of light assaulted me and it took a moment for my eyesight to adjust. We stood in a room the size of Hole. Everywhere I looked seemed like a soft place to fall. The sofa and chairs were covered in crushed velvet and the floorboards were hidden by a layer of fluffy carpet. Even the tables had rounded edges.

A tall woman strode toward us. Her round cheeks were bordered by auburn curls. She curtsied when she reached us.

"Welcome back, Your Highness."

"Thank you for accommodating us on such short notice," he replied.

I became transfixed by the smattering of freckles across the bridge of her nose.

"It's the freckles, isn't it?" the woman said, smiling. "A rare sight, I know."

Callan motioned between us. "London Hayes, Knight of Boudica, meet Fenella, Daughter of Persephone."

I nodded. "Nice to meet you."

Fenella looked me up and down. "A real knight. How about that?"

"How do you keep this place hidden?" I asked. "I saw the marker to the entrance, but it still seems as far away now as when I first spotted it."

"A trick of the light, my dear." She smiled at her own joke. "Murdina will be out in a moment with a hot meal for you."

"Thank you."

Callan steered me to a comfortable sofa and I sank against the soft cushions. It felt good to go boneless.

Fenella positioned herself in the chair adjacent to us.

"What kind of witches are you?" I asked.

"Our magic differs. Mine is summoning. Murdina's is fire. Our common bond isn't just magic though. It's our love for vampires." She set an affectionate hand on Callan's arm. "His mother was a particular favorite."

"So how does it work?" I asked. Vampires were insular by nature and the laws regarding dhampirs made them unlikely to mate or marry outside their species.

Fenella's brown eyes fastened on me. "If you're asking whether we're a coven of magical concubines, the answer is no."

Callan ran his hands up and down his thighs. "Oh, I don't know. Magical concubines has a nice ring to it."

My elbow slipped straight into his ribs. Oops.

The aroma of freshly baked bread wafted over and a stout woman appeared carrying a tray of food.

"Bless you, Murdina," Callan said.

"Anything for you, Your Highness." She lowered the tray to the table in front of us. "He's still as bonny as ever." She winked at me and made herself scarce.

I began to salivate at the sight of so much scrumptious food on one tray. A bowl of berries. Cooked carrots. Salted green beans. There were even a few legs of meat I couldn't identify, not that I'd eat it.

I gestured to the tray. "How do you manage all this bounty in the middle of nowhere?"

Fenella clasped her hands around her knee. "Being a Daughter of Persephone has its perks."

"You mean having a special relationship with vampires has its perks," I said.

"We do have a sort-of favored nation status," Fenella admitted, "but we're a very capable coven. Vampires rely on witches for a reason. After all, we're the motor that keeps the earth chugging along."

She wasn't wrong. Without magic, the world would've succumbed to its wounds long ago.

"And this sanctuary." I waved a hand. "Who is it for?"

"Whoever is in need, of course. We don't discriminate in the same way we ask that others not discriminate against us for our choices."

Point taken.

Fenella pinched a berry from the bowl and popped it into her mouth. "I need to check on Godfrey and make sure he returned safely to the stable. Enjoy your meal."

"I will, thanks."

Fenella stooped to kiss Callan's cheek before striding to the door.

I speared a carrot and devoured it. After a few more hungry bites, I realized that Callan was watching me.

"Aren't you going to eat anything?" I imagined they stored blood for the vampires they worshipped. Interesting that they didn't offer any to him. Maybe they knew his secret. I couldn't decide whether that annoyed me or pleased me.

His gaze remained pinned on me. "I'm enjoying the view too much to stop and eat."

I stopped chewing and swallowed awkwardly. He handed me a glass of water, anticipating my cough.

I drank. "You have to stop saying things like that if you want us to stay apart in Britannia City."

His face softened. "I'm sorry about that. I thought I was keeping you safe, but I see now that's a mere fantasy." He edged closer. "And there are so many better ones to explore."

"I don't know. Maybe staying apart is the right call. With Maeron threatening me..." I shrugged. "Family dinners could be uncomfortable."

He ran his fingers though my hair. "I could murder him. What did he think I would do when I found out?"

"I assume he was prepared to lie to cover his tracks."

He kissed the top of my head and released me. I took the opportunity to spear a few green beans and eat.

"Tell me more about his plan," Callan said.

"Here's what I know: he lied about what Romeo told him as well as how Romeo died. He's in possession of the book that went missing from the curator's office at the museum and he destroyed pages from books in the library to keep anyone from learning the information he'd discovered."

A muscle in his cheek pulsed. "I dislike being lied to."

"Doesn't everybody?" I kept my own lies to myself. One crisis at a time.

Callan picked up a leg and ripped off a layer of meat. "I knew he was interested in the Immortality Stone from the time we were boys, so I don't suppose it should surprise me that he wants the stone from the wolves."

I debated whether to share my thoughts on the subject. Sharing treasonous thoughts with a vampire prince seemed like a very bad idea. Then again, I seemed full of bad ideas these days.

"I think he intends to use them to seize control of the throne," I blurted. Caution whipped straight into the wind. Didn't even float a little first.

Callan barked a laugh. "You can't be serious. Usurp his own father?"

"Have you read any history books? That's standard fare."

"I think your mother might've overdone your lessons. Maeron adores our father."

"He also hates Imogen."

"Certainly not."

"You're blind, Callan. He despises Imogen and he's angry with his father for replacing his mother so quickly."

"Father had no choice. It was for the good of the realm."

"There's always a choice. And Maeron is still a scared little boy who lost his mother at a young age. He wants to make her proud."

"You and I lost our mothers, yet we've made no plans to overthrow anyone." His eye twitched. Subtle, but I saw it.

I swallowed a mouthful of carrots. "Callan, what are you not telling me?"

"What do you mean?" He tore more meat from the bone and chewed.

I dropped my fork and it clattered on the plate. "Whatever it is, tell me."

Slowly he set down the drumstick. "The truth will endanger you."

"The truth will protect me," I said, recalling my conversation with the tortoise. Different topic, similar result.

He licked his lips, debating. "Perhaps you're right. The fact that we're in Scotland only increases the risk."

"Increases? I thought we were okay in Wales. Why should Scotland be worse?"

"The reason I stayed away—that I wanted to keep us apart—is because of my father."

I took a long drink of water, digesting the news. "Glendon or Casek?" There was only one acceptable answer.

"Glendon."

I relaxed, but only slightly. "Why would you be in danger from your own father?"

Callan's jaw set. "My father didn't send me to House Lewis to honor the peace treaty."

"You mean you volunteered?"

"No." He offered a derisive snort. "There was no such thing as volunteering. My father commanded my every move." He drew a deep breath. "Delivering me as King Casek's ward was part of a larger plan."

A bad feeling settled in the pit of my stomach. "A plan you've been aware of from the beginning?"

He glanced around the room and dropped his voice. "He's been playing the long game. Before I was handed over, he invited me for a private chat. I was aware of the treaty negotiations, but I never believed he would actually relinquish his own son."

His only son. Callan was the sole heir to House Duncan. It seemed incredible from any standpoint that King Glendon would've agreed. A larger plan made sense.

"How did you react when he told you?"

"At first I was hurt. Then angry. He waited until the anger unleashed to reveal the rest of his plan."

I looked at him sideways. "Why would he wait?"

"Because he wanted to see my loyalty to House Duncan on display. To know he'd made the right decision to send me away."

"Because Birmingham wasn't enough? He felt it necessary to test you again?" Even though it was twenty years later, I was angry for him.

Callan lowered his head and I felt the sting of guilt for raising a difficult subject.

"I'm sorry," I said. "I shouldn't have mentioned it."

"No, you're absolutely right. The king is cold and calculating, always has been. I'm nothing more than a pawn to him. He only wants to groom me for the throne in order to preserve his own legacy should his immortality be cut short like Britannia's."

I let the news simmer. "It's been twenty years and you haven't made a move. What were his orders?"

"I've made moves."

Despite the heavy topic, I laughed. "What moves? You live in the palace and the family adores you."

He offered an embarrassed smile. "All part of the plan. Ingratiate myself first. Become a trusted member of the family."

"You got that far."

He nodded. "It wasn't hard. They were more lovely and welcoming than I expected. Before I met them, I believed Casek was like my own father. Different territory, same ruthlessness."

"But they surprised you?"

"Even Maeron was more tolerant than I anticipated. I'd assumed one of us would end up killing the other by the time all was said and done."

"But instead you became like true brothers."

"We fight like blood brothers, that's for certain. And I

can't always trust him to do the right thing." He gave me a pointed look. "Although I still don't see him plotting to overthrow our father. That's a bridge too far even for Maeron."

"What exactly did King Glendon instruct you to do?"

"Steal the Immortality Stone and return to Scotland with it."

I whistled. "Is that what he was after during the Battle of Britannia?"

"He never said as much, but I believe it was. When his attack failed, he had Plan B ready to be executed. I was originally meant to wait until the terms of the treaty were up and smuggle the stone to Scotland."

"He doesn't want unrest."

Callan shook his head. "He wants everything to be handled quietly. Remove the stone, honor the treaty. That way when he finally takes power, he'll face less resistance from the general population. It's not as though the stones are common knowledge and House Lewis won't want to suggest to the public that the only reason they're as powerful as they are is down to a single stone."

Callan wasn't joking about playing the long game. It was one of the advantages of being an immortal vampire. No wonder he was determined to remove Britannia from the throne. She might've lived forever if she hadn't died during the battle. Britannia with silver hair. I shuddered. Even knowing it was impossible, the idea still terrified me.

"But your father asked you to act sooner? Why?"

"I don't know. He sent a messenger to tell me. That's the reason I was being followed, and the reason I decided to stay away from you. Casek may have won the battle, but Glendon is far from finished with the war."

I wondered whether Glendon knew that more stones

had been unearthed. It wouldn't surprise me to learn he had a mole—even more than one mole—in House Lewis.

"Why would you worry about my safety?"

He exhaled. "Because I refused to steal the stone and return to Scotland, which meant his next step would be to persuade me through other means."

And I would be the other means.

"He's no fool," Callan continued. "He's kept tabs on me all these years. And I've had to send reports on my progress with the family. Show evidence of how I've convinced them to accept me as one of them."

"But he didn't ask for evidence to show your loyalty to House Duncan over the years?"

Hesitation flickered in his eyes. "He has, and I've found ways to appease him."

It was a lot to unpack. "When did you decide to disobey him?"

"A long time ago. I was only a boy, but I recognized the difference in the way I was treated. Glendon never treated me like a son. Hell, he didn't even treat me like a living being. I decided that when the time came, I'd stand up to him and refuse to do his bidding."

"But you haven't shared his plan with anyone in House Lewis?"

He winced. "I worry that such a revelation would ignite a war. I don't want to be responsible for any further bloodshed. I've contributed quite enough of that."

"I think we might be headed for war either way. Just because Glendon intends to take over without bloodshed doesn't mean House Lewis will let that happen. And what about House Peyton? Won't it make them nervous to see House Duncan expanding their territory?"

Callan's expression was solemn. "Knowing my father, he's made contingency plans."

It suddenly occurred to me what those contingency plans might be.

"What is it?" Callan asked in response to my opposite-of-a-poker face.

"Davina."

He snarled. "I would never let him hurt Davina."

"I'm not talking about hurting her. I'm talking about marrying her. Merging Houses would be a way of legitimizing the takeover and appeasing the public."

Davina was the obvious option. Imogen was older and, therefore, tougher to mold. She also lacked the Lewis bloodline, whereas Davina had both Lewis and Osmond blood in her veins.

"My father could've taken a bride for the past two decades," Callan argued.

"Exactly. Why has he waited? If you're right about him playing the long game, it makes sense to wait until a certain princess had come of age."

Rage simmered behind Callan's eyes. "I won't allow it."

A memory sparked in my mind. "Princess Louise."

"What about her?"

"Do you think she might be one of your father's contingency plans?"

Callan mulled it over. "I thought I was the contingency plan. That he intends to match me with Louise. I suppose either one would be a bone to throw House Peyton in order to get them to support House Duncan."

In some ways the second option was worse. It made Davina expendable.

It made my sister expendable.

Callan squeezed my hand. "Let me deal with Glendon. The priority is getting you home safely."

It was time to peel off a layer of protection. With everything he'd just divulged, I owed him at least this much.

"No. The priority is the same as when I got here." And it seemed even more pressing in light of our conversation. "I need to find the Spirit Stone before anyone else."

He glanced at me sharply. "The Spirit Stone?"

"I've been trying to learn more about the stones. That's why I went to Wales." I told him about Friseal's Temple and the two remaining stones. "The information led me here. The Spirit Stone is somewhere on the Isle of Skye. That's where I was headed when you found me."

I felt a twinge of guilt for not disclosing my possession of the Elemental Stone and the Transcendence Stone, but I'd share that intel when the time was right. If Callan ended up in the king's clutches, I couldn't risk Glendon discovering my involvement.

"I believe you mean when I rescued you." He wore a faint smile. "I'll join your quest. We'll recover the stone together and keep it from the king's hands."

"No, I can't ask you to do that. I got myself into this. I'll go alone."

"You take on far too much. You should have backup."

"What if your father finds you here?" I glanced around at the sanctuary. "You're in his territory because of me." If anything happened to him, it would be my fault.

"He won't."

I inclined my head. "What about the Shades?"

"The Daughters of Persephone hate my father. They would never betray me."

"They love vampires so much they created an entire organization devoted to it, yet they hate your father?"

"Just because they love and revere vampires doesn't mean they fail to recognize the stench of the rotten ones." He gnawed the last of the meat from the bone. "Besides, they don't need to know our destination. I'll get us there without their help. I know this land like the palm of my hand."

"Does anyone really study the lines on their palm with that kind of focus?"

He laughed. "Have I mentioned how much I've missed you?"

I let myself get lost in a haze of emerald. "I wouldn't mind hearing it more than once."

He pressed his lips to mine. "I've missed you, London Hayes. More than I believed was possible."

Part of me wanted to confess all my secrets this very moment. I forced myself to lock the vault and choke on the key.

"I'm glad you're here," I croaked.

"How could I resist a damsel in distress?"

"I didn't need your help at the river. I'd basically made it to land."

"Whatever you say." He plucked a berry from the bowl and tossed it into my mouth as it opened to object.

I tasted the sweet juice and decided to forgive him. How could I hold a grudge against someone who'd fed me multiple times?

Fenella returned to the room. She brushed twigs from her hair. "Godfrey was in a mood."

"I don't suppose you have another mode of transport we could use," Callan said. "One less moody, perhaps."

Fenella aimed a finger at him. "For you I'd wrestle a dragon to the ground and demand obedience."

"That seems unnecessary," he said. "Anything less volatile?"

She broke into a broad smile. "Would an enchanted coach do?"

Callan's lips parted to reveal his impressive fangs. "Perfect."

Fenella motioned to the tray. "You two finish up. I want you leaving here with full bellies. I'll get Bessie ready and meet you between the oaks where you left Godfrey."

"There's a chance we won't be able to return the coach to you," Callan warned.

"I told you, Bessie's enchanted. She knows the way home." Fenella turned on her heel and left the room.

I gave the other leg to Callan and cleared the remainder of the food from my plate. It felt good to share a secret with him. It felt even better to kiss him again. When he first told me we had to stay away from each other in Britannia City, I had no idea whether we'd see each other again. I'd convinced myself that he didn't care enough. Or at all.

For once I was happy to be wrong.

14

The coach was a turquoise Volkswagen van with the name 'Bessie' spray-painted across the side in pastel pink letters.

"Why Bessie?" I asked.

"Fenella's mother was called Elizabeth. I assume it's named for her."

"Do me a favor. If you ever name anything after me, let it be cooler than a van."

"How about a city? Will that do?"

"I think that's already been done."

I climbed into the passenger seat. "I'll let you drive this time."

Callan settled behind the wheel. "I believe Bessie will be doing the driving." He tapped the wheel. "Enchanted, remember?"

Fenella tapped on the window and it lowered automatically. "Don't worry about Bessie. You tell her where you're headed and she'll choose the best route to get you there." Her gaze flicked to Callan. "And by best, I mean the safest."

He nodded. "We are in your debt, Fenella."

"Nonsense. I do this in honor of your mother. It was lovely to meet you, London. Take care of our prince."

The window rolled up.

"Bessie, please take us to the Isle of Skye," I said.

The van's engine roared to life and off we went.

It felt strange that neither one of us had to focus on directions or our surroundings. We only had to pay attention to each other, which had its advantages. I was almost disappointed when Bessie came to a stop.

"It feels like we've only been driving for thirty minutes," I said.

"That's the beauty of an enchanted coach. No idea how long it really took."

We climbed outside. It became quickly apparent that we'd arrived across the water from our destination.

Callan looked at Bessie. "I don't suppose you convert to a boat."

Bessie's motor purred in response.

"Didn't think so."

Lights twinkled in the distance, beckoning me. "No bridge?"

"Not anymore," Callan said. "I should have remembered."

"It's been a long time since you've been home." He'd lived in Britannia City longer than he'd lived in Scotland. No wonder he felt more at home there.

"At one time there was a bridge that connected Skye to the Highlands, but it was destroyed during the Great Eruption. Every attempt to rebuild since then was interrupted, either by a monster or a group of islanders reluctant to receive visitors."

Or maybe by a powerful stone that hoped to remain hidden?

"What do you suggest?" I asked.

"You're the water witch. Can't you part it like the Red Sea so we can walk across?"

I could, except I had no idea what kind of creatures we'd encounter along the way. Given my experiences in Scottish waters so far, I wasn't excited to find out.

"I'd like to see what's behind door number two, please."

He grinned. "I'm sure we can commandeer a fishing boat if we keep walking."

"And leave some poor soul without his livelihood? No thanks." I'd rather find another way.

I put my hands on my hips and glanced skyward. Golden eagles still inhabited this region. Two of those would be strong enough to carry us across. Unfortunately there was no sign of one eagle, let alone two. I reached out with my mind to see whether any suitable animals roamed the coastline. Sea or air would do.

Callan looked at me. "Magic carpet ride?"

"I'm not a genie."

I brushed against a mind and probed a bit more. Nope. A red deer was no use to us.

The sound of wings flapping grabbed my attention. A birdlike woman hovered above the ground to my left. A sharp beak protruded from an otherwise humanoid face. Reddish-brown hair crowned her head. Her black wings beat against the air.

A harpy.

Callan instinctively bared his fangs, but I quickly stepped in front of him to block the harpy's view.

"Need a lift?" she asked.

I was relieved to hear her friendly tone. I wasn't in the mood to fight.

"That would be helpful," I said.

She looked me up and down. "What have you got to trade? I need your most prized possession." She glanced at Callan over my head. "I take it he's not up for grabs."

Scowling, he emerged from my shadow. "I'm a..."

"Vampire. No kidding." The harpy dropped to the earth and planted her feet on solid ground. "We don't get a lot of your kind out this way. I thought it might be fun to take you for a ride." She arched a suggestive eyebrow.

"You don't get a lot of vampires?"

"We call this area the Land of Misfit Supernaturals. We basically carved out a vampire-free zone without angering any actual vampires."

"That's all very interesting, but I'm still not bartering my friend," I said. The name Callan seemed too dangerous to utter now that I knew about the king's plan. I'd have to be careful.

"Fair enough. You've got something better to offer anyway. I was only willing to make an exception because he's so yummy."

Callan looked at me askance. "What else could you have that's better than me?"

"Nothing," I said quickly.

The harpy folded her arms and slammed her wings shut. "No treasure. No ride."

I cast a glance at the island. Maybe there was an alternate way.

I sighed. There was no time to waste. I wasn't the only one hunting for the stone and I could easily lose my advantage.

I reached into my pocket and removed the ripe plum I'd taken from the castle. "Here. This is mine."

The harpy smiled at the small purple fruit in my palm. "So it is." She accepted the plum and I winced when she bit into the soft flesh. "Delicious. I'll savor every bite and you'll watch me."

"Why do I need to watch you?" I asked. "You've got the plum."

She licked the plum's skin. "Deal or no deal."

I handed over my prized possession. Those three minutes were excruciating. It was like watching someone destroy one of my happiest memories.

As though sensing my despair, Callan whispered, "We can always find more food."

He didn't understand and I wasn't in the mood to explain. I simply nodded.

Once the harpy finished, she spat the pit on the ground and spread her wings. "Who's first?"

"We go together," I said.

Her gaze flickered between us. "Too much weight. I have to separate you."

"Liar," I shot back. A harpy her size was capable of lifting a woolly mammoth if one decided to make an appearance.

The harpy glowered at me. "Very well then." She held out both hands and snapped her fingers. "Let's hope I don't drop one of you into the shark-infested waters."

I hesitated. "What about the return journey?"

"That isn't what you bargained for, lass." She grabbed our hands and rose into the air before I could argue. The power of a free market economy.

As we sailed over the choppy water, I was grateful to have found the air option, despite her attitude. My gaze met Callan's and he offered an encouraging smile. I felt myself instantly relax. How did I go from absolute terror at the sight of him to feeling soothed by his presence, like I could handle any obstacle thrown in front of me? What a strange world I inhabited.

The harpy released us without bothering to land. "Have fun. You might want to steer clear of the giant. He's grumpy when he's hungry."

I glanced up at her. "What giant?"

She hovered out of reach. "Oh, did I forget to mention him? Good luck!" Her dark wings flapped until she blended with the night.

"We can handle a giant between us," Callan said, unperturbed.

"I'm glad one of us is optimistic."

I scanned the jagged peninsula. "This place is gorgeous." There was just enough light emanating from the island to see the hills as a backdrop to the rolling plains.

Callan pointed to the east. "I see a village. We should start there."

No.

The word thrummed in my mind over and over like a steady heartbeat.

I gave voice to the thought. "No."

He gave me a perplexed look. "You have a better idea?"

Use the Force.

The Force is always with you.

I'd thought the tortoise was being funny, but I was beginning to realize it was more than an amusing pop culture reference. If I could use my magic to connect to the stone, I could pinpoint its location—or at least land us in the general vicinity. It was worth a try. As handy as a treasure map would be with an X marks the spot, I didn't see one materializing any time soon.

I took a moment to connect with my magic and concentrate. "East."

Callan didn't question it. "East it is."

The pulsation continued to draw me toward it. We walked in silence so that I could focus on the sensations.

"Why is it that you can sense the stone's energy?" Callan finally asked.

"I'm sure I'm not the only one." I didn't want Callan to think too hard and start developing theories. There was too much I was unable—or unwilling—to explain.

"If there were others, they would've discovered the stone by now," he said.

"And so would I, except I didn't know what I was feeling or how to interpret it."

"At least you don't need to rely on eyesight to find the way."

He was right. The island was dark, although not as dark as the land around the sanctuary. There were signs of life here, however compact.

I changed the subject before I felt compelled to confess everything. "If I share a thought with you..." I trailed off. Okay, maybe this was the wrong kind of distraction. I couldn't possibly say the words out loud, could I? They were treasonous and I had no idea how Callan would react. Just because I believed he'd listen didn't mean I was right. I could be delusional. Wouldn't be the first time.

Interest sparked in the vampire's eyes. "How would you categorize this thought? Naughty or nice?"

I cleared my throat. "It's not what you think."

"How disappointing."

The truth shall set him free—if it didn't kill me first.

I inhaled courage through both nostrils. "Something we discussed at the sanctuary reminded me of a theory I've been researching."

"About the stones?"

"No. About the battle. I think your father—pardon, your *fathers*—might have conspired to kill Queen Britannia."

His expression remained placid. "You wouldn't be the first to harbor such thoughts, although you might be the first to voice them to a member of the royal family. What makes you say this?"

"Britannia was unstoppable. House Duncan wasn't ready to admit defeat at that point and your father made one last stand in the city. House Lewis won, yet she died. No one saw what happened. One minute she was beating back your troops and the next minute Casek was declaring victory and announcing a treaty, *but the queen was dead*."

"That's the whole reason Casek moved as swiftly as he did to secure the treaty. He didn't want to give Glendon a chance to regroup in light of her death."

"And why didn't Glendon seize the moment? Britannia was the tactical genius. The real powerhouse of House Lewis. Your father is smart and conniving. Do you really believe he'd simply acquiesce at that point? It doesn't fit."

"And you think what does fit is that the kings plotted to murder her. What would be in it for House Duncan? He gained nothing."

"As you said, he's been playing the long game. He removed his main obstacle and lived to try another day."

He scowled. "And that other day is upon us."

"It fits with everything you told me."

He shook his head. "Father wouldn't do that though. He loved Britannia. Even more than that, he's far too honorable."

I thought of Casek's affair with my mother. "Even the most honorable among us can act in a way that's disappointing to others. Without knowing the reasons, we shouldn't judge." Okay, maybe I was talking a little about me, too.

Callan's voice cut through the whirling dervish that was my mind. "Now I have a question for you. Why was the plum so important to you?"

"What?"

"I was there, London. The harpy identified that plum as your treasure and I doubt it was because it was the only food you carried."

I stared at the ground as we walked. He'd shared so much with me and I'd kept my secrets buried. Surely I could spare this one piece of myself. "It reminded me of something special."

He tilted his head and studied me. "Something or someone?"

"My mother."

He nodded. "It would've rotted anyway if you weren't willing to eat it."

"It was enchanted. Anyway, I only wanted to savor the memory a bit longer."

I picked up the pace to get ahead of him so he couldn't see my face. It felt too exposed. I'd been taught that any vulnerability would get me killed. It was hard to unlearn that at thirty.

Callan's long legs quickly caught up to mine. "I'm sorry you had to give it up."

I shrugged. "The stone is more important than reliving a childhood memory."

"Have you always put everyone else's needs ahead of your own?"

"It isn't like that. The stone is crucial. In the wrong hands..."

"I know."

I wish I could tell her how much she means to me.

I frowned. "Excuse me?"

"I didn't say anything." *I've already said more than I should have. I've endangered us both.*

My heart hammered in my chest. It was the influence of the Spirit Stone. It had to be. The spirit encompassed powers like mind control and telepathy. I was someone who possessed all the powers combined so it made sense that the stone would impact me in some way. The genetic material was there, ready to tap.

"Stay calm, but I need you to cloak your thoughts," I said.

He halted. "Sorry?"

"I can hear them." I pointed to his head. "Your thoughts."

His eyebrows crept up. "You can read minds?"

"Not usually, but I think the Spirit Stone is triggering that ability. I can manipulate animals so some element of spirit powers already flows through my veins."

"I'll do my best."

"Please." I didn't want to know what he was thinking. Well, that wasn't strictly true, but it was for the best to remain ignorant. Callan's thoughts would be too distracting and I still had too much work to do. There was the small matter of smuggling the stone home and placing it with the others in my secret dimension. I'd have to come up with a plausible excuse for not handing over the stone to Callan. He'd be on board with not telling Maeron, but that didn't mean he'd be keen to let me keep it.

Callan eyed me closely. "What number am I thinking of?"

"Twenty-one."

His smile faded. "What was the first gift I ever bought Davina?"

"A music box. It was pink and played Chopin."

His expression turned grim. "Right. Cloaking it is."

"You didn't believe me?"

"I thought you might be exaggerating."

"Because I exaggerate so often?" I shook my head. "And here I thought you knew me."

His hand grabbed mine. "I do know you, London. More than I'd like to sometimes."

I tugged my hand away. "Gee, thanks."

"That's not how I mean it."

"I know, I know. You want to keep me safe and knowing me makes us both vulnerable."

"It's true."

It was true. We were cut from the same cloth. No wonder we got along so well.

"Don't read my mind," he said.

"I'm not."

He pointed to my eyes. "I can see your eyes shifting. That's your tell."

I laughed. "I have a tell?"

He zigzagged a finger from one eye to the other. "Shifty eyes."

"You're ridiculous." And gorgeous. And funny. Sheesh. Good thing he couldn't read *my* mind. I felt embarrassed listening to my own thoughts.

A powerful pulse of energy nearly knocked me off my feet. I stumbled to the side and regained my balance.

Callan grabbed my elbow to steady me. "Everything okay?"

I turned. A sheet of water cascaded from a cliff into a pool below. It was reminiscent of Orkney and I wondered whether it was a coincidence. That if I'd stayed in the portal as long as I was supposed to, I would've emerged right here.

"There. That's where the energy is coming from."

"The water?"

"The cove."

There was a cove hidden behind the waterfall but the entrance was large enough to spot through the curtain of water that spilled from the cliff.

"How do we reach it?" Callan asked.

Good question. The cove was behind the waterfall and the only access point seemed to be from the cliff above. Even that would prove difficult. I considered freezing the waterfall and sliding down icicles to reach the cove, but that would make returning to the clifftop too hard. My axe and daggers wouldn't be the right tools either. As impressive as Callan's fangs were, I highly doubted Callan would be eager to use them as ice picks.

The sight of a golden eagle lifted my spirits. Better late than never. I reached out with my mind and latched on. The bird resisted but only mildly.

"Found us a ride," I said, as the eagle swooped toward us. A second eagle appeared right behind his friend and I tapped into his mind too.

"Preferable to the harpy." Callan rubbed his wrist. "I swear she dug her claws into me on purpose."

"Better than what she wanted to do to you."

The eagles carried us across the pool of water and cut through the waterfall. We landed in the mouth of the cove and the eagles swooped in a circle and flew back the way they came.

I wasn't sure what I was expecting, but it certainly wasn't the naked giant stretched out in front of me. I'll say this much—not everything about him lived up to his name.

"I think we might be at the wrong address," Callan whispered.

The sound echoed in the damp chamber.

One eye popped open and the giant grunted.

"Did I say I'd take door number two? I meant door number three." Despite the joke, I couldn't leave. The stone was somewhere in this cove. I felt it with every fiber of my being.

Realizing his company wasn't a dream, the giant sat up and flashed a broad smile.

I gasped. One of his top teeth was significantly smaller than the others and my stomach plummeted as I recognized the symbol etched in the hard surface.

The giant had the stone—*in his mouth*? "Are you kidding me?" I looked at my companion. "Please tell me you're seeing this."

Callan raked a hand through his hair. "I should've guessed."

"You should've guessed a giant is using an ancient powerful stone as a cap? I don't think anybody's that clever."

"It explains why no one's experienced the stone's influence the way they did with the wolf stone. Between the secluded location and the giant's mouth, it's been pretty well hidden."

Who knew how long the giant had been using it as a replacement tooth or where he'd even discovered it?

The giant shifted to his feet and lumbered forward.

"He looks happy to see us," Callan surmised.

I groaned. "If he says fee fi fo fum, I'm out of here."

"I'm sure that's merely a stereotype. Whatever he says, you'll play along because that's our only hope of getting that stone," Callan whispered.

He was right. I wasn't about to kill the giant simply for

choosing the wrong dental work. Just because he had a reputation for being grumpy didn't mean he deserved to die. If that were true, half the dwarf population of Britannia City would be dead.

I gathered my courage and beamed at the giant. "Hello. I'm Lincoln and this is my friend, Washington."

"It's the other way around," Callan whispered.

I ignored him. "We were told in the village that you're the expert on island history."

The giant's eyebrows rose slightly, as though he was surprised to learn this about himself. "Brandon knows."

"Who's Brandon?" I asked.

The giant pointed to himself.

Ah, got it.

"I've made it a rule never to trust anyone who talks about himself in the third person," Callan said under his breath.

"We don't have to trust him," I hissed. We were plotting to steal the giant's tooth. I wasn't worried about developing a tight bond.

The earth trembled as Brandon approached us. "You want to know about Skye?"

"I do." The more I considered it, the more I realized it was true. What an amazing opportunity to learn about the island from one of its earliest inhabitants. Of course Brandon had probably been forced to live out of sight prior to the Great Eruption, but that didn't mean his knowledge would be lacking. My mother would've given her left arm for a chance like this. Of course, a giant pair of trousers would make the whole experience more palatable.

The giant jabbed a finger in Callan's direction. "And you?"

"Yes, me too," Callan said. "I'm eager to learn."

The giant appeared pleased by the response. "Brandon has never left Eilean a' Cheò."

"You've been here a very long time then," I said. Which meant the stone had been here a very long time as well.

He nodded. "Home."

For a fleeting moment, I let myself wonder what it was like to have one place to call home. This island was his sanctuary. I lived in a flat in Britannia City that I called home, but I could hardly think of it as a sanctuary, certainly not while I lived each day in fear.

"Where is your home?" Brandon asked.

I cut a quick glance at Callan. It was a hard question for him too.

Callan tapped his chest. "In here."

The giant squinted, confused. "Brandon doesn't understand."

"Home is love," the vampire said. "That way I can take it with me wherever I go."

I must've stared at him for a beat too long because he shot me a quizzical look.

"You must really love it here," I said to the giant. I didn't want to get distracted by my feelings right now. There was too much at stake and I was too much of a grownup to get swept away by emotions.

Most of the time.

"Can you blame him?" Callan interrupted. "He has everything he needs right here. A place to sleep, plenty to eat. Isn't that right, Brandon?"

The giant smiled and I glimpsed the stone again. I felt a pang of guilt for planning to relieve him of a tooth, but he had plenty of others. And if he managed to replace it once, he could do it again.

Dinner, a voice said. *Brandon hungry.*

Uh oh. The giant wasn't as dumb as he sounded. Not when he was smart enough to hide his thoughts about eating us.

We had to hurry.

Invisible? Callan's voice popped into my head. *I figured you wouldn't want me to cloak these thoughts.*

It helped that we could both turn invisible, although it was still risky. The giant would be able to feel us, which meant he'd be able to hurt us. Unconscious would be better.

I looked around for a boulder or something heavy we could use to knock him out without killing him. The giant's furnishings were basically nonexistent.

Brandon stepped closer and the floor of the cove rumbled in response.

I had to act now. I connected to my magic and gathered the air around me. I pushed it forward with as much force as I could muster and blew the giant back against the stony wall.

"I'll hold him. You get the stone," I said.

Callan glanced at the naked giant. "You don't expect me to use that as a step stool, do you?"

"I don't care what you use. Just hurry." I held out my hands and concentrated on keeping the giant's arms and legs pinned to the wall.

Callan used the crags in the cove wall to gain purchase and climbed as high as the giant's shoulder.

The giant turned his head and snapped his teeth. I was able to keep his arms and legs immobile using the force of air, but I couldn't do anything about his mouth.

"Can't you use your spirit powers?" the vampire yelled over the sound of rushing air.

"If you could read his mind, you'd realize how useless that suggestion is."

I ran through a mental list of other abilities connected to the spirit. Was there one I could try to connect with?

"On the count of three, stop the wind," Callan said. He hovered on the stone wall like a spider waiting to attack its prey.

"Okay."

"One. Two. Three." The Beast of Birmingham leapt to the giant's shoulder and clocked his cheek. Hard. The giant's head jerked and slammed against the wall. In that single move, I glimpsed the vampire that terrorized Birmingham and reduced walls to rubble.

An object shot from the giant's mouth.

The Spirit Stone.

Callan jumped to the floor, grabbed the stone, and ran toward the exit. I raced after him.

Footsteps thundered behind me, shaking the cove so hard that rocks cascaded down the walls. There would be no time to wait for the eagles. We ran straight through the gushing water and jumped.

My feet hit the water first. The icy temperature sank straight through the boots to my skin. If I made it back to the Circus, I'd put in a request for footwear made out of the same material as my armor.

Ahead of me I spotted Callan's powerful strokes as he swam toward shore. A large splash told me the giant had decided to give chase. Terrific.

I reached out with my mind for any nearby aquatic life. I didn't bother to check their species. I pulled them all to the giant. Animal magnetism at its best.

I reached for my magic and felt the key slide into the lock and click open. The water was mine to command. I created a current to give my arms and legs a rest. I turned onto my back for a glimpse of the giant. He'd been waylaid by a school of fish. There were so many gathered that they formed a wall between us. I switched back to my stomach and skimmed the water's surface until I caught up with Callan on land. He had the stone tucked under his arm.

"Not the most elegant execution of a plan," he remarked.

"Nobody's grading us. We need to hurry. The fish won't hold him back for long."

Callan and I dashed across rocks until we reached solid ground.

"We need to get off the island. He won't follow us to the Highlands," I said.

"What makes you so certain?"

"He told us he's never left Skye. He won't start now." Not for a tooth.

"Good point."

We ran until we reached the nearest beach. No boat in sight. Now what?

The roar of the giant shook the ground beneath our feet.

"You take the stone," Callan said. "I'll hold him off."

"Absolutely not. We're leaving together."

He smirked. "You think I can't handle myself?"

"I think I'm not the kind of person who would leave you here to become a snack for an angry giant."

"Ah, so you'd take anyone. In other words I'm not special."

I cut a glance over my shoulder. "Seriously? Do we have to do this now?"

He grinned. "Tell me why you want me to come with you."

"Because I don't want you to be eaten. Is that so hard to understand?"

"Admit it. You care about me." His lopsided smile was infuriating.

I opened my mouth, ready to admit just how much I cared.

An enormous fist launched Callan into the water. For a giant, he'd proven surprisingly stealthy.

The giant zoomed past me in pursuit of Callan. He must've been able to tell the vampire had possession of the stone. That, or it was payback for Callan's punch in the cove.

I chased the giant and launched an attack of my own. I pulled the air toward me in an attempt to slow the giant's steps and give Callan time to escape. I saw no sign of the vampire. Then again, it was difficult to see past the huge hunk of flesh called Brandon.

The giant was proving too strong for the wind. I'd caught him off-guard in the cove, but he was ready for me now. His defenses were up and he was laser-focused on Callan and the stone.

I debated using water magic, but I couldn't risk drowning Callan. Same with earth magic. Without knowing Callan's whereabouts, I could end up hurting him *and* losing the stone to the sea.

I pulled at the sand like it was a carpet as the giant attempted to cross it on his way to the water's edge. At that moment, Callan's head surfaced and he thrust the stone out of the water in triumph. He must've dropped it and gone diving to retrieve it.

Which also meant he was oblivious to the giant's proximity.

I raced to the shoreline. "Callan, swim!"

It was too late. The giant reached him in two strides, creating dual fountains with each step. He grabbed Callan around the waist and began to shake him. The vampire's eyes rolled to the back of his head and he dropped the stone into the water. The giant was too overtaken by anger to notice. He continued to shake Callan like an angry toddler whose favorite toy had been taken.

My heart thumped wildly. If I didn't do something, Callan would die. I abandoned the stone and let it succumb to the waves.

Callan was in danger. I had to save him.

"Brandon, look at me!"

The giant turned, his arm still outstretched, and I unleashed chaos.

Silver light exploded from my hands and streaked toward him. The giant shot backward like he'd been fired from a cannon. Callan slipped from his grip and fell into the water. The giant landed on his back with a huge splash. I waited to see whether he emerged from the water to try again, but the waves quickly grew calm. Brandon remained still.

I waded into the water and dragged Callan to shore. Then I went back for the stone. I followed the steady beat of the thrumming until I located it wedged between two oversized shells.

By the time I returned to the beach, Callan's eyes were open and he was back on his feet.

Thank the gods.

I tossed him the stone. "Good save."

Unsmiling, he caught the stone. "You're still glowing silver."

A quick glance at my hands confirmed the statement.

"What happened to you?" he asked. "That light..."

I faltered.

"I've heard stories, but I've never seen it with my own two eyes."

"It's magic, Callan. Only magic."

Bitterness spilled from his lips. "Only magic? Are you even a witch?"

"On my mother's side."

His frown deepened. "And your father's?"

I hesitated. The moment I dreaded was finally here.

"London, what was your father?"

"He was a vampire."

He stared at me. "You're a..." He couldn't even bring himself to say the words.

"That's right, Your Highness. I'm a dhampir."

15

Callan stared at me with a mixture of revulsion and regret. "A dhampir? How?"

"I assume you know how half breeds are made. Same as any other baby."

He scowled. "Don't mock me. Not now." Pain etched his handsome features and I felt a pang of guilt. "I confessed everything to you about my father." He jerked away, seemingly unable to make eye contact with me. I didn't blame him. He was right. He'd shared his deepest, darkest secret with me and I'd failed to reciprocate.

"I'm sorry."

"This is why you avoid vampires," he continued. "It's all starting to make sense now. Why someone with your talents would hide. You could be living comfortably on the House Lewis payroll, but that would've drawn too much attention to you."

"I don't go out of my way to kill vampires."

"Maybe not, but you're lethal to us."

"And *you're* lethal to *us*."

The pain on his face intensified. "Do you truly think I would ever hurt you?"

"This isn't about you. There are many other vampires in the world and every single one of them would view me as a major threat. If you reveal the truth about me, you're signing my death warrant."

He looked as though I'd slapped him. "You think I would do that?"

I threw out my hands in frustration. "I don't know what you would do. You're not just a vampire. You're royal. You have obligations to two Houses and to the vampires you rule over."

"After everything we've been through, you still don't trust me." His voice was barely audible, but I heard the injection of sorrow in each note.

"While we're on the subject of trust, why haven't you told me about your plan to mass produce synthetic blood?" It was a lame attempt at deflection, but I couldn't help myself.

His green eyes lost their luster. "Who told you? Adwin?"

"I read your mind," I lied. "Seems I'm not the only one keeping secrets."

"Yes, I have plans to one day eliminate the need for human blood. To close all the tribute centers. Does that make you happy? Does that make you less likely to see me as an enemy?"

"I *don't* see you as an enemy." I grabbed his hands, but he wrenched them away.

"You talk about the ambitions of my brother and my fathers, but you're just as guilty. Even worse, because you pretend to be different."

"I don't pretend. I *am* different." I pointed to the stone.

"That isn't about ambition for me. This is about the safety of the realm. The *world*."

His face reddened with anger. "Because no vampire can be trusted with power. Isn't that right?"

I fell silent. Yes and no didn't seem like the right answer.

"My mother gave me one goal in life—survive. I've spent the past thirty years figuring out the best way to do just that. She sacrificed everything for me. The least I can do is try."

"Then I suppose I'll let you get on with it. Far be it for me to stand in your way. Take your precious stone. That's obviously the most important thing to you." He thrust the stone into my hand.

I gaped at him. "You're leaving?"

"We'll only endanger each other if we stay together. We're like oil and water."

"That isn't true."

He regarded me. "If you truly believed that, you would've told me."

"Don't leave because you're angry."

His eyes softened. "I'm not angry."

My eyebrows lifted. "If you say 'just disappointed,' I might slap you with my magic."

The absence of a smile broke my heart. "Good luck, Hayes," he said. "I hope you get the outcome you want."

"At least let me help you cross the water to the mainland."

He grunted. "Do you seriously think I can't manage without you? You forget who I am, London Hayes."

I didn't watch him leave. Instead I turned away and tried to convince myself it didn't matter. I was here to do a job that was much bigger than the two of us.

I called to a golden eagle and had it carry me across the water to the mainland. I kept the stone tucked in my bra. I looked like I had a third boob, but deformity was a small price to pay for keeping it safe.

I landed on the ground in a standing position and looked around for Bessie's silhouette. The odds were good that I'd beaten Callan off the island so the enchanted coach should still be in the vicinity. I decided to leave Bessie for Callan. Given his confession, he was in more danger in Scotland than I was. I'd find another way home.

My skin began to itch like crazy and I whipped around expecting to see Callan. Instead two vampires marched toward me. They wore the uniform of House Duncan.

Terrific. The glam squad was here.

"I'm so glad I ran into you. I am completely lost." I pretended to scan the area. "I'm supposed to meet my husband, but I think I'm in the wrong place."

The taller vampire sniffed the air between us. "You reek of seaweed."

I offered a sheepish grin. "I may have fallen into water." Once or twice.

"There were reports of a bright light coming from this area," the second soldier said. "See anything?"

"Yes. I think it came from over there." I pointed to the island.

The tall vampire scrutinized me. "What's that bulge in your chest?"

How rude.

"This?" I tapped the stone. "A memento of my visit to Skye. I like to collect trinkets from places I've been."

Something's off about her.

I'd like to collect her as a trinket.

A voice rang out behind them. "That's the one! Don't let her leave."

Three more vampires emerged from the shadows all in House Duncan colors.

"I'm afraid you've mistaken me for someone else," I said.

"The van's right over there, just where she said it would be," the third vampire said. His gaze raked over me. "And this one fits the description."

Murdina wasn't kidding about her. She looks like an Amazon.

It seemed at least one of the Daughters of Persephone wasn't as loyal to Callan as he believed.

"Where's your companion?" the newcomer asked.

"She said she was lost and was supposed to meet her husband," the tall vampire interjected.

"I bet that's him," the third vampire said.

I didn't reach for Babe. I went straight to magic. The explosion on Skye would've exhausted an average witch. Good thing I wasn't average.

I jammed my hands downward and activated my earth magic. The ground trembled and split. Two soldiers lost their balance and toppled over. I pushed both hands forward and conjured a blast of wind to blow the remaining three soldiers backward.

The two vampires on the ground scrambled to their feet and bared their fangs. They sprang toward me at the same time and I fended off their advance with a sweeping gesture. Magic rushed from me like a geyser and forced them off their feet.

If I could keep them off balance long enough to reach Bessie, I could escape. I didn't want to leave Callan without wheels, but I knew he was right when he said he could manage without me. He wasn't a foot soldier. He was the Demon of House Duncan. The Highland Reckoning.

He didn't need me.

I scanned the shadows for Bessie and spotted her

outline in the distance. I glanced at the five soldiers nursing their wounds as they struggled to their feet.

I could make it.

I sprinted toward the enchanted coach.

One hundred yards.

Seventy-five.

Fifty.

I'd never run this fast in my life. My legs were likely to catch fire if they moved any faster.

A hard object slammed against the bone of my ankle and I stumbled. Regaining my balance, I glanced down to see glowing golden chains. I tried to leapfrog over them, but they twisted around my ankles. I raised my hands to blast them off and another set of chains wrapped around my wrists and held them together.

My attempt to connect to my magic was met with a blank wall. A barrier had slid into place effectively blocking me from reaching it.

I turned toward my attackers to see two cloaked figures approached me with the five vampires marching behind them.

"What are these?" I demanded.

The figures lowered their hoods. "Anti-magic chains."

I looked straight into a set of familiar eyes.

"Sorry, lass," Fenella said. "Things have changed since Callan was a wee lad."

At least she had the decency to sound genuinely sorry. Murdina looked downright gleeful.

"The king will pay a handsome fee for you," Murdina said. "And our coven is in dire need of coin."

"What about Callan?" I asked.

Murdina smiled. "Don't need him if we got you. The king will be most pleased."

"I thought you hated him."

"Someone's had to keep his bed warm over the years," Murdina said. "We take turns and in return he keeps us from starvation."

My face hardened. "The queen was your friend."

Fenella bowed her head. "We do what we must to survive. You're still young. You'll learn."

I yanked on the chains but to no avail.

"There's no point in struggling," Murdina said. "The chains prevent you from accessing your magic. Trust me, they've been tested extensively."

I felt sorry for the witches offered up as test subjects.

Murdina stepped forward and tugged the stone from my suit. "This radiates power." She examined the markings. "What is it?"

"Mine," I hissed. I strained against the chains. I couldn't let the king have that stone.

"It must be very special if you keep it with you," Murdina mused.

She didn't seem to know anything about the stone. For all she knew, I'd brought it with me from Britannia City. If they were close to the stone for long enough, they might figure out—until I remembered Fenella say that she was a summoner and Murdina was a fire witch. If that was true, the Spirit Stone would have no impact on them unless they had spirit magic in their genes to trigger its power.

"I believe it's the reason they went to Skye," Fenella said.

"Now that you mention it, I heard them whispering about stones." Murdina hefted the stone in her hand. "Is that what you came for?"

The tall soldier joined Murdina. "The king might want to see this."

I swiveled toward Fenella and whispered, "Please take

the stone somewhere safe. Wrap it in chains like these. Whatever you do, do not give it to the king."

Fenella swiped the stone from Murdina's hand. "Careful, lad. This is a witch's weapon. It'll kill a vampire with a single touch. We'll take this to the king so no one gets hurt. Can't have your blood on my conscience."

The soldier didn't object. "Fine with me. We've got the bigger prize to deliver." He leered at me.

Regret seeped into my pores. I'd never felt so defeated. I managed to lose both Callan and the stone. For all I knew, Fenella would deliver the stone straight to Glendon in order to curry favor. I'd done what I could though. I had to accept the outcome.

For now.

The soldier ripped Babe from the sheath and the blunt end of the axe made contact with my skull. My teeth rattled.

"That's for knocking me over. Twice." He turned to his men. "Load her up. She can't hurt you now."

"We'll take care of the coach," Fenella said.

The tall vampire bowed slightly. "The king thanks you for your service, ladies."

Murdina winked. "Oh, he thanks me every Thursday night."

"Thanks for the visual," I muttered.

"Thanks for the next six months' wages," Murdina shot back.

Two soldiers flanked me and marched toward a cluster of motorcycles. I didn't have magic, but that didn't mean I was without skills.

I reached my bound wrists up and over the nearest vampire's head and pulled the chains taut against his neck.

"Let me go or I'll kill him," I growled.

The tall vampire laughed. "And then what? Trip and fall

as you attempt to flee?" He gestured to the chains around my ankles. "You'd waddle like a penguin."

The other vampires joined his laughter. I tightened my hold on the vampire's neck and he started to choke.

The laughter stopped.

The soldier still holding my axe swaggered over and gave me a sharp look. "Release him now."

"Make me," I ground out.

"Easy enough." He raised the handle of the axe and whacked me on the back of the head.

My fingers slipped away from the chains and my head throbbed with pain. A metallic taste filled my mouth as my body slumped against the hostage. I couldn't defend myself. I couldn't even stand.

My eyes slammed closed and I gave myself over to the void.

16

Heavy eyelids slid open to see a pair of black boots lined up with my mouth. One swift kick and I'd lose my teeth. I lifted my gaze to view my captor. He was over six feet, although it was hard to tell exactly how many inches from my position on the floor. His reddish-blond hair was slicked back away from his unlined face. A few strands of silver glistened in the dim light. Although his face was unfamiliar, I'd recognize those green eyes anywhere.

"Your Majesty," I said, wincing. My head was still sore.

King Glendon looked down his nose at me. "You recognize me?"

"Yes, Your Majesty." The formal address tasted sour in my mouth.

"Have we met before?"

"No." *I know your son*. Although Callan no longer wanted to know me. Even if he knew where I was, he'd leave me to rot in his father's dungeon. I glanced around to confirm my location. Yep. I was in a dirty cell the size of a shoebox. Well, I was accustomed to small living quarters. I could make it work.

The king hooked his thumbs around the top edges of his jacket pockets. "Are you an assassin? Because if you are, you're not a very good one."

Still wearing the golden chains, I shifted to a seated position and leaned my back against the stone wall. "I'm not an assassin, so you can dispense with the chains." It was a long shot but worth a try.

Unsurprisingly the king ignored the suggestion. "Do you know how many have tried and failed?" His gaze lingered. "Women, too. You wouldn't be the first, you know."

Maybe not, but I'd be the last. I kept that thought to myself. No reason to give him pause.

"I'm not here to kill you."

He cocked his head. "You have an accent."

"I'm from Britannia City."

He frowned. "You travel without a pass. How?"

"Magic."

He grunted. "I'd like to know how your magic bypassed my defenses."

I managed a smile. "Maybe over a drink sometime."

The king observed me with calculating eyes. I'd seen that look often enough. He was taking the measure of me.

"Why are you in my realm?" he finally asked.

No violent reaction. It was a solid start. "I'm a Knight of Boudica. I'm here on behalf of my banner." A partial truth.

"A knight, you say?"

"Yes."

"London Hayes. That's your name, isn't it?"

It didn't surprise me that he knew. Callan said the king's spies had been making notes and reporting back to him.

The king scrutinized my outfit. "Interesting armor for a knight. I suppose it's infused with magic."

"Yes, Your Majesty."

"Our knights wear traditional armor."

He might've just as well said real men don't wear pink. His attitude didn't surprise me. From what I knew of him, King Glendon struck me as a vampire steeped in tradition.

"I suppose they carry lances and ride around on steeds too." The king probably had a low tolerance for sass, but I couldn't help myself. If I was going to end up on a torture rack, I might as well enjoy myself first.

His expression remained inscrutable. "Where is my son?"

"And who might that be?"

"Don't play with me, child. I am not as inept as my soldiers."

I snickered. "They do fall down pretty easily."

The king crouched down to address me. "Answer me, child. Why are you in Scotland with my son?"

"It was meant to be a romantic getaway. House Lewis doesn't like that Callan has chosen a witch as his mistress. They think I'm beneath him."

"And they would be correct." He snapped his fingers and two guards appeared on either side of him. "Show our guest to the main reception hall. Be sure to keep her chains on. I'll join you momentarily."

Part of me worried he'd join me with a small army, but I didn't think he'd go to the trouble of sending me to a reception hall if he intended to kill me. Not right now, anyway.

The guards escorted me along a long, narrow corridor. The air was heavy with damp and reeked of stale urine.

"Lovely perfume you're wearing," I said to the guard on my left.

He snarled but said nothing. We arrived at a spiral stone staircase and made our way up. The thud of our boots echoed with each step. Not an avenue to travel in secret. We crested the steps and immediately entered a great hall. The middle of the dome-like ceiling was lined with wooden beams that featured antler-inspired chandeliers. Kami would've called the room's overall design 'mountain man chic.'

There were no portraits on the wall, at least in this room. No statues of the king or his idols. No personal touches of any kind, including evidence of a son and heir.

We passed several doorways until we reached an arched wooden door. The door opened from the inside.

"Go on then," the left guard urged.

I crossed the threshold and the door closed behind me. A single rectangular table took pride of place in the center of the room. It was covered in platters of fruit, cheese, and bread.

A vampire pulled out a chair adjacent to the head of the table and gestured for me to sit. I put her at roughly mid-forties. She had the kind of miserable face that made you wonder what troubles she'd endured in her lifetime.

"Thank you," I said.

"You won't be thanking me before long," she whispered. She slammed a plate on the table in front of me and stalked out of the room.

Alrighty then.

The king entered the hall a moment later and the first thing I noticed was the long length of his stride. He moved like Callan. The air escaped my lungs as the reality settled in. This vampire was Callan's father. The devious vampire who wanted to steal the Immortality Stone and overthrow House Lewis.

I popped to my feet, nearly knocking over my chair in the process. Although I wasn't keen on genuflecting for vampire royalty, I recognized the need to play along. Anything to find a way out of this mess.

"Sit. You must be hungry. You look like a dog that's been left chained outside to a post."

I held up my bound wrists. "Gee, I can't imagine why."

He pushed the platter of fruit closer so my T-Rex arms could reach it. No plums, unfortunately. I chose an apple instead, rolling it toward me until I could palm it in one hand and raise it to my mouth. No small feat. If the situation weren't so dire, I'd pause to be impressed.

King Glendon sat in the chair adjacent to mine. The second his bottom hit the seat, the door swung open again and a bevy of staff streamed into the room carrying a variety of offerings. Bottles of crimson liquid. A teapot. The sight of cupcakes made my mouth water. I couldn't remember the last time I ate a cupcake. My mother had been alive, so that gave me an inkling.

As though sensing my enthusiasm, the server set a cupcake on my empty plate. The cupcake was topped with creamy frosting and it took all my restraint not to lick the top clean. There was the small matter of my dignity.

"Eat before I change my mind," the king ordered.

He didn't mince words.

The staff vacated the room as quickly as they'd swarmed the table. The king's goblet was filled to the brim with blood and mine was filled with water. I hadn't noticed anyone pour from the bottles.

"Not that I'm complaining, but why are you bothering to play host when we both know I'm going straight to the dungeon?"

"I find that people are more open and honest when they're well-fed."

And here I'd expected the torture rack.

"What am I being open and honest about?" I stuffed a quarter of the cupcake into my mouth and relished the sweet taste. Great gods above. My mother always referred to sugar as the white devil, but right now I didn't even care if the cupcake was hexed. It was sinfully delicious.

"Tell me about this banner of yours. The Knights of Bootlaces?"

"Boudica." I swallowed the mouthful of cupcake. "You've heard of the warrior queen, haven't you? Fought valiantly against a Roman invasion?"

His green eyes twinkled with amusement and I averted my gaze. Those eyes were too familiar. I had to remind myself not to be fooled—the vampire beside me was nothing like his son.

Nothing.

"I've heard the tale."

"It isn't a tale. It's an historical fact." I shoved the remaining section of cupcake into my mouth before the king could change his mind about feeding me.

"I have no issue with women in warfare. If I had a daughter, I would've raised her alongside my son."

Except you didn't raise your son. Not even a little bit.

"You wouldn't have forced her to marry instead?" For a traditional vampire, I found his statement questionable. It was possible he was trying to manipulate me by appealing to my feminist views.

"Heavens, no. I would've raised her for battle like many high-born girls in the Middle Ages. Imagine what I could've accomplished with a brood of warrior children." His gaze traveled around the room. "I'd be seated in Buckingham Palace by now, I can promise you that."

"What's wrong with this place? Seems nice enough. A bit minimalist for my taste, but to each his own."

"To each his own." He grunted. "My mother used to say that when she disapproved of something. It's one of those statements that's meant to appear tolerant yet reeks of judgment."

A sliver of insight into King Glendon's background. Duly noted, Your Majesty.

"Once upon a time, a knight was more than an occupation. It indicated social ranking," he said.

"Yes, I'm aware. Are you familiar with the Knights Templar?"

He sniffed his disdain. "Christian knights, weren't they?"

"Yes, and they admitted women as knights."

He snatched a chunk of cheese from a nearby platter and tossed it into his mouth. "I suppose you worship the likes of Eleanor of Aquitaine."

"I don't worship anyone. Besides, she wore armor but she didn't actually fight."

A smile tugged at the corners of his mouth, revealing the tips of his fangs. They were like two shark fins that promised violence just beneath the surface.

"Where did you learn all this history? I've been told the educational system in Britannia City is utter shite."

"My mother was a history teacher." I saw no point in hiding that basic fact.

"I see. And your father?"

"Don't know. Never met him."

He drank from his goblet and used the back of his hand to wipe away the beads of blood that remained on his upper lip. "Why a knight? Why not defense or agricultural work? That would've provided a more secure lifestyle."

"I was young and directionless. That's what happens when you're an orphan at a young age."

Nodding, he raised his goblet to his mouth. "You learned to defend yourself early on, I gather."

He had no idea. "Yes."

"I don't see any scars. Fought many monsters, have you?"

"More than I can count."

"Is that because you're not very good at mathematics?" He chuckled as he lowered his goblet to the table. "I jest."

There was a certain charm to the king, I'd give him that. No chance in hell I trusted him though.

"I leave the counting to our office manager." Minka was drawn to numbers like a raccoon to a dumpster.

The king observed me over the rim of his goblet. "So your banner has sent you all the way to the ends of the earth for what? What quest could be so important that you would enter a foreign territory illegally?"

"I was on a romantic getaway with your son, remember?"

"I remember the lie, yes. Why aren't you together now?"

"We had a fight."

"A lovers' quarrel. Such drama at your age. Much easier to simply devise a schedule and set expectations from the beginning." He drank again, draining the glass. Before he could set it down, a staff member emerged from the shadows and whisked the goblet away. "What did you argue about?"

"I want to marry him. He said no."

"Making demands of a royal vampire. Cheeky."

"I suppose you have his bride all picked out."

The king smiled. "As a matter of fact, I do. I have great plans for my son." He leaned forward. "Which is why I'd very much like to find him."

I shrugged. "I wish I could help you. I'm not sure he wants anything more to do with me, so if your plan is to use me to lure him here, it's not going to work."

He answered with a smile so deadly, I felt compelled to close my eyes. "No, little dove. I have other plans for you." Calmly, he ran the linen napkin across his lips. Then he snapped his fingers and a woman appeared in the hall as though she'd been awaiting her turn. "Prepare our guest for her new chambers, would you, Cynthia?"

Cynthia raised her arms and her sleeves slid back to reveal two wrinkled hands. Her unlined face suggested early middle age but the pruned skin of her hands said otherwise. She made small movements with her hands until they began to glow with a red and orange light.

My chair slid back until it reached the wall and an unseen force lifted me to an upright position.

"Been doing this a long time, huh?" I asked through gritted teeth. Whatever she was doing to me made it difficult to move my muscles, including my facial ones.

Cynthia ignored me.

"It must be tiring to only be asked to do one thing over and over. Boring too." My eyes darted to the king. "I bet he doesn't pay well either. Strikes me as a cheapskate."

Cynthia didn't take the bait. She kept weaving her magic web.

"You don't want to do this," I told her.

Her eyes met mine and it was then that I saw it. An acknowledgement. Maybe she recognized me as one of her own. Maybe she felt sorry for me because she hated the king. Whatever the reason, I sensed I'd struck a nerve.

Not that it mattered.

"She's ready," Cynthia proclaimed.

Ready for what?

"Take her to the tower," the king said. His tone was so mild; he could've just as easily been requesting a side of bacon with his eggs.

Guards appeared and took me by the arms. They dragged me along a different corridor and up a long, spiraling staircase, which was no easy trip considering my ankles were still bound by anti-magic chains.

"It wouldn't be a castle without one of these, would it, boys?"

The vampires ignored me.

We arrived at a gleaming gray door that looked solid enough to stop a train. They escorted me into the room and released me. There was no handle on the other side of the door. Not really a surprise. This wasn't a room designed to be exited voluntarily.

"Don't bother trying to use magic once your chains are off," the guard said. "Won't work."

My gaze flicked to the metal door. "Enchanted door?"

"Enchanted tower," he replied. "That's what Cynthia does. Preps you for the tower so the enchantment works on you."

"And if that fails, there's always the hungry dragon that flies around outside looking for scraps," the second guard added. "An extra layer of security."

They laughed uproariously like it was the funniest joke they'd ever heard. Still chuckling, they left the room and slammed the door shut.

On cue my anti-magic chains dropped to the floor. I kicked them aside and tested the potency of the enchantment. Just as they claimed, I couldn't connect with my magic. Dammit.

My gaze swept the interior. There were no windows and the only source of light came from a pathetic bulb that dangled high above me. A single mattress took up the center of the floor. No blanket. There was, however, a pot to piss in —such luxury.

I was trapped in an enchanted tower in a foreign land with no way out and no one to save me.

I'd never see Kami again. My best friend would have to find another partner with whom to fight monsters. The other knights were just as capable, of course, but nobody knew Kami like I did. Nobody shared our history. Two teenagers living in the forgotten bones of a Tube system beneath a sprawling city. We'd been through hell and back together and we were still standing. Still fighting the good fight.

Gods, what would happen to the menagerie? The banner would take them in. They'd have to. Minka was a pain in the ass, but she wasn't heartless. She'd take pity on Big Red, Hera, and the rest of them. The other knights would each take one home—wouldn't they?

There were questions I'd want answered. Would Briar embrace the backbone I knew she was hiding? Would Neera finally find love? Would Ione establish her independence from her older sister and start working cases without her?

What about Davina and Casek? They'd never learn the truth about me. Would they care?

So many questions.

My gut felt like it was being sliced open for the universe's amusement.

I'd never see Callan again. My heart tightened at the miserable thought. If I died, we'd never get to resolve our fight. He'd be angry with me for the rest of his immortal life and hate himself for not letting go of it.

I didn't want him to suffer. Yes, he was a vampire and, yes, I was a dhampir, but that didn't mean we had to be enemies. Kendall Masters was molded into a weapon to wage war on those who'd wronged her family. She didn't act on instinct. She was taught to lose control.

I'd been taught the opposite.

My mother made certain that I honed my skills *and* learned to control them. She instilled me with compassion and a sense of responsibility. It was plain from the visions I'd had at Atheneum that she and my father had deeply loved each other. If she could fall in love with a vampire, then so could I. And if King Casek could fall in love with a witch...

I pushed down the anguish and studied the walls of my dark prison. I should've been smarter. That would teach me. Or it wouldn't—because I'd be dead. My mother would be furious at the mistakes I'd made. They were foolish and they were enough to cost me my life.

For a moment I considered being one of those people who believed in an afterlife. *At least I'll be reunited with my mother again*, I'd tell myself soothingly. But I knew that was bullshit. Dead was dead. My body would be burned or carted outside the city along with all the other corpses this week, unless King Glendon handled his dead subjects some other way.

I sagged against the cool stones of the wall and sank to the floor. There'd be no knight on a white horse to save me, not when I was both the princess and the knight.

Gods above, I was an actual princess imprisoned in an actual tower.

Except this was no fairytale.

* * *

Be sure not to miss **One Knight Stand**, the fourth and final book in the *Midnight Empire: The Tower* series.